To F

the story and ...
place where its set.

Niki Sepsas
2-13-04

SONG OF THE GYPSY

Niki Sepsas

ATHENA PRESS
LONDON

ISBN 1 932077 05 7

First Published 2003 by
ATHENA PRESS
Queen's House, 2 Holly Road
Twickenham TW1 4EG
United Kingdom

Printed for Athena Press

SONG OF THE GYPSY

After silence, that which comes nearest to expressing the inexpressible is music.

Aldous Huxley

Acknowledgements

There are a number of people to whom I would like to express my heartfelt thanks for their invaluable assistance in this work.

To the loving memory of my father and mother, Dean and Christine Sepsas, to whom I dedicate this story.

To my sister and brother-in-law, Christy and Bucky Wood, who provided much of the motivation and all of the technical support for the project.

To George C. Sarris and Peter Gerontakis of Birmingham, Alabama, cherished friends to whom I looked in creating the principal male character in the story.

To George's sister, Joanne, and her husband, Ted, in Tsitalia, Greece, whose family served as the model for most of the characters in the story.

To the residents of the tiny village of Tsitalia who have opened their hearts and their homes to me on my numerous visits to the area. It was their village that served as the setting for this story.

To Peggy in Houston, who believed in me and to my numerous friends, who encouraged me along the way.

To my English teachers at Phillips High School in Birmingham, who suffered with me over the years and provided encouragement and inspiration.

And last, but certainly not least, to "Erika", the central figure of the story. She need not be identified. She does exist, and, more importantly, knows that she is the person with whom I would love to search for the perfect sunset. An unattainable dream, she will forever hold this writer's heart.

Chapter One

"It's on that column in the back, about three feet from the bottom," he said.

Turning to face him, she squinted into a brilliant Mediterranean sun. "Excuse me?" she replied.

"Lord Byron's signature on the column. That is what you're looking for, isn't it?"

"I'm not sure what I'm looking for is any of your business," she countered, slightly annoyed. "But since you mention it, that is what I came here to find. What gave me away?"

A smile streaked across his tanned mahogany face.

"It might be the guidebook you're holding," he suggested. "Plus the sun hat and the camera bag."

"There are a lot of other tourists here. How did you know I was American?"

"The shoes. Definitely not European. But I apologize for intruding. It was rude of me."

She softened just a bit. "I apologize also," she said. "I didn't mean to snap at you. I had a bad experience yesterday with a cab driver in Athens. My name is Erika Johanssen," she said, extending her hand.

"Chris Pappas," he replied, shaking the outstretched hand. "It's nice to meet you."

She released his hand and pushed back a shock of blonde hair which the breeze, despite her sun hat, was scattering across her face. The shoulder length shag haircut framed a face with high cheekbones, Windex-blue eyes, and a slightly turned up nose. A shy half-smile revealed a string of teeth that belonged in a toothpaste commercial. A swan-like, aquiline neck tapered into the trademark square shoulders of competitive swimmers. Her arms were long, slender, and well defined. It appeared that her only concession to the cosmetic industry was a splash of crimson across her lips and a hint of eye shadow. A blue short sleeved

9

cotton cover up hung just over her hips, and a pair of white denim shorts accentuated legs that obviously spent a lot of time on a bike or treadmill. The chiseled features and healthy glow gave her the appearance of the quintessential rosy-cheeked Southern California surfer girl turned forty-something.

"The name definitely sounds Greek," she said, "but I think I detect a bit of a Southern drawl. What part of the States are you from?"

"Now who's playing investigator?" he smiled. They both laughed as they walked to the end of the white marble columns dazzling in the sun-glow of late afternoon. "But you're right. I was born in Fairhope, Alabama. My parents emigrated from Greece."

"Good Lord! I travel a good bit with my job, but I've never been to Alabama. Never even met anyone from your state. Were your parents from this area?"

"No, they were born in a village south of here in the Peloponnese. Here's the signature you're looking for." He pointed to the weathered carving of a name in the massive Doric column.

"Just 'Byron'?" she asked puzzled. "Seems pretty simple for such a complicated man. Was he really a lord?"

"George Gordon was his real name. He inherited his title when his grand-uncle died."

"But why did he choose to carve his name here at Cape Sounion? My book doesn't say anything about that. Seems like this place is really out of the way."

"It is," he explained, "but Byron loved it. He came to Greece in 1824 with a passion for liberty, and threw himself into the Greeks' struggle for independence. He felt he could come to a no more noble end than to fall on the battlefield fighting alongside the Greeks for their freedom. It's ironic that he died of a fever soon after he arrived in the country. Tourists have been leaving graffiti on these columns at Sounion since the days of the Roman legions. Look at some of these dates." He pointed to dozens of names of long-forgotten travelers who over the ages felt compelled to scrawl a message into the twelve marble pillars overlooking the Mediterranean shimmering cobalt blue almost

200 feet below.

"This is the southernmost tip of the Attican peninsula," Chris continued. "It's the last point of land the ancient Greeks saw as they sailed away on their voyages and the first point they saw on their return. That's why they built the Temple of Poseidon, the god of the sea, on this spot about five centuries before Christ. All that's left now are these twelve columns. But all that should be in your guidebook."

"It's not," she replied.

"Looks like you've been cheated then. What does it tell you about Sounion?"

"It says that the Taverna Dionysius over there is the best place to escape the heat with a cold soda. And that's just about what I'm ready to do."

"Only if you like being overcharged. It's pretty much on the tourist trail. The white awning place just at the head of the bay is the neighborhood joint where most of the locals go. They wander in when they wake up from their siestas in the afternoon and have their coffee, ouzo, and grilled octopus."

"Sounds awful," she frowned.

"Actually it's quite good when it's cooked properly. The fishermen beat them on the rocks a minimum of 100 times to tenderize them. Otherwise they're like chewing rubber. They grill them with lemon juice and oregano."

"You're sounding like a guidebook now," she quipped.

He flashed the smile again. "Sorry, I got a little carried away. I really do enjoy this place though. It's said to be one of the most photographed views in the Mediterranean at sunset."

She turned towards the sun-dazzled sea, and suddenly became silent and pensive. The sun, though still at least two hours from being swallowed by the Mediterranean, burned with a fiery brilliance even now in early May.

"I've got a pocketful of drachmas if you'd like to try the octopus," he suggested. "It's almost time for the locals to start arriving."

"I really didn't come here looking for company," Erika said, still looking out over the ocean. "Actually, just the opposite. I'm looking for some time by myself." Her mood had grown serious, and she seemed transported to another time and place. Chris sensed the change.

"I understand," he said. "Sorry for the intrusion. Have a pleasant trip."

Erika was still staring hypnotically at the ocean when Chris shouldered his pack and headed down the hill towards the coffee shops and *tavernas*. He couldn't resist a last look at her. Leaning back against the giant stone column, the breeze dancing through her blonde hair and rippling the flowing cotton cover-up she wore over her shorts, he thought she was positively stunning. Almost a postcard.

That's worth a picture, he thought as he pulled his Nikon from his pack and adjusted the setting for a silhouette—shooting into the sun with the girl outlined alongside the pillars of the temple. Shifting slightly to his left, he was able to capture a sunburst between the columns. A goddess in her temple, he mused, returning the camera to his pack and zipping the compartments shut.

He was still thinking about her as he continued his hike down the hill toward the coffee shop a quarter mile away. The strings of lights running along the awning's anchor ropes had been turned on, and he could hear the faint sounds of Greek music wafting through the cassette player.

Shuffling along the dirt road, he was still daydreaming about the brief encounter when a white Toyota Corolla pulled up alongside him.

"Decided to take you up on the refreshment offer if it still stands," the voice said as she rolled down the window. Erika appeared somewhat cheerful now, with even the hint of a smile straining to make an appearance on her face. She had returned from her mental journey and seemed even more beautiful now than when they had talked at the ruins.

"You bet," Chris replied trying to suppress his surprise and excitement at seeing her again. "And I promise not to sound like a tourist brochure."

"Get in then, it's a deal."

Chris flipped his pack into the back seat and slid into the Toyota.

"Do you not have a car?" Erika asked, steering the Toyota back on to the road. "How did you get here—the bus?"

"It's really not that bad a trip," Chris answered. "Takes a little more than an hour from Athens if the traffic's not too heavy. A little longer on the return because all the beach people are heading back to town."

She turned the Toyota into a gravel parking area surrounding the scruffy-looking awning strung about 100 feet from the semi-circular bay of Cape Sounion, whose water looked to be too clear to even support the weight of someone's gaze upon it. At some time in the distant past the weathered canvas must have been white, but years of sun, dust, wind, and neglect had rendered it a dingy gray. Open on all sides, the makeshift tavern consisted of about a dozen dilapidated card tables with equally dilapidated folding chairs in various stages of decay scattered among them. The entire operation looked like it could have been blown away at just the rumor of a storm.

Just outside, in the shade of a smaller awning, was a massive barbecue grill fashioned from a black fifty-five-gallon oil drum. A grizzled old man with a sleeveless white undershirt and a ponderous belly flopping over his gray flannel pants fanned a pile of glowing charcoal into life. With his black sailor's hat cocked rakishly over his forehead, he could have passed for Anthony Quinn's Zorba. He smiled at Chris and Erika as they entered the café.

"*Peraste, kirie,*" a young man said greeting them at the entrance. "You like this table?" he asked switching to English. "Very nice view of bay."

"That will be fine," Chris said, as he and Erika sat down at a table with a white plastic covering. The young man gave the plastic a quick wipe with his towel, and a young boy appeared with napkins and silverware.

"It will be a few minutes before the octopus is ready," Chris said. "Would you like to try an ouzo?"

"I've heard it's the Greeks' answer to tequila," Erika smiled, "but I guess I'll have to try one."

"*Dio ouzakia me nero,*" Chris said to the waiter in Greek. The man nodded and quietly vanished behind a curtain separating the food preparation area from the rest of the *taverna*.

"Sounds like you still do pretty well with the language," Erika said. "Do your parents still speak Greek at home?"

"That's about all they spoke up until the time they died. Never learned more than a few sentences in English. My grandparents spoke no English at all."

Erika noticed a slightly faraway look in his eyes as he talked about his family. She imagined him coming from the typically large extended family unit common among Mediterranean people. Grandparents, aunts, uncles, cousins. Probably all very close. She felt a slight pang of jealousy as that was something she had always wanted herself, but never had when she was growing up.

"So," he said, leaning back in his folding chair, "was there anything besides Lord Byron that brought you to Greece?"

"Just a vacation," she replied. "I've been to Europe before but never to Greece. A friend was supposed to come with me, but she trashed her ankle skiing in Tahoe last February."

"You said earlier that you travel for a living," he said.

"I do. Mostly in the States, though. I'm a photographer for *Western Woman* magazine."

"You came to the right place then. Tremendous photo ops here in Greece."

"Actually, this kind of shooting is pretty new to me. I do product photography for the magazine. Mostly indoor shots of kitchens, food, table settings and such with lights, a stylist, and all that. I've never done much in the way of scenics, but I've always wanted to. This trip is giving me a great chance."

The waiter reappeared with two glasses of ouzo, a decanter of ice water, and two empty glasses. He placed them on the table and turned to leave. On his way back to the kitchen he stamped his foot at a scrawny gray cat that was cautiously peeking into the shade of the tent. The animal bolted across the parking lot.

"What's the program here?" Erika asked picking up the glass of ouzo. "Do you shoot this or is it sipped?"

"Definitely sip it," Chris said. "But first let me do this." With his spoon he fished an ice cube out of the water pitcher and dropped it into her drink and did the same for his. The liquid slowly turned a milky white.

"Looks dangerous," Erika said, sniffing the drink. "Smells kind of like medicine."

"It's a licorice-based liqueur. Smells a little funky but tastes pretty good over ice. It's been said that only a country with a mountain full of gods could have given the world a drink such as this."

Chris raised his glass and looked at her. "To temples and sunsets," he said.

She smiled and looked into his eyes as she raised her drink. He still sported the roguish grin and his black onyx eyes had an impish twinkle. She studied for a moment his deeply tanned face where the first traces of crow's feet and faint lines were beginning to appear around the eyes. A shock of curly black hair tumbled carelessly from under the edges of his faded baseball cap. She thought he must be in his mid-40s, but he looked to be in good physical condition, with broad shoulders and a back that tapered to a small waist. His most noticeable features were his arms. Even in his loose fitting blue T-shirt, his biceps appeared to be large and tight, and his triceps ran in long, sinewy knots to his lower arm. The forearms were just as heavily muscled. A silver chain around his neck vanished under his T-shirt. Probably a patron saint, she thought. The overall image was of a person who had spent much of his life outdoors.

"Temples and sunsets," Erika said. She sipped her drink and made a face. "It's definitely a sipper, but are the ice and water okay here?"

"Safe as home. You won't have a problem with the water anywhere in Greece."

Erika settled back in her chair and appeared to be much more at ease than she had been earlier. The day in the sun had brushed her face a light pink that became a perfect canvas against which her eyes sparkled. Chris thought they were the most stunning things about her. They had a brilliant intensity and a piercing blue opaqueness, like the eyes of a Malamute. Try as he might to avoid staring, they drew his own eyes back to them like a moth to a flame.

A number of locals had wandered into the taverna and were

welcomed by the waiter, who knew each of them by name. Two families with small children pulled together two tables near the entrance, and an elderly couple sat down at a table next to Chris and Erika. The old man had a head full of thick, gray hair and a huge mustache that spread across a lined face that appeared to be a tapestry for the history of Greece. He sat bolt upright in his chair with his gnarled hands draped over a carved walking stick that had covered many a dusty mile with its owner. The old lady was short, slight, and wore a black dress with a black shawl wrapped around her shoulders. Her hair was solid silver. Looking at Chris and Erika, she smiled and nodded her head.

Erika looked back at Chris. "What about you?" she asked. "Are you on vacation?"

"Sort of. My cousin in the village is getting married next week and I came over for the wedding. Decided to spend a few days before and after."

"What do you do when you're not prowling around ancient ruins?"

"I'm a writer," he replied. "I freelance for magazines."

"Really?" she said seeming somewhat surprised. "I'm not sure I would have made that connection. What type of articles?"

"Mostly travel features. No *National Geographics* or anything. Airline, travel, and adventure magazines. Stuff like that."

"Interesting," Erika said. Chris noticed her shifting in her chair, as if she was now slightly more interested in conversation. She leaned forward somewhat curiously, and he caught the scent of her hair. A fresh, subtle smell that reminded him of clothes just taken out of a drier in which a lightly scented static cling sheet had been inserted.

She began asking him questions about where he had been published. Did he freelance full time? Were there any major features in his portfolio? His answers were short. His mind was racing, imagining that something could be happening that he wanted very much to happen. Did she seem more than a little interested? Was it all just informal chit-chat? The more she spoke, the more he found himself becoming entranced. Steady, boy, he thought. Don't get carried away. It's just an afternoon drink with an attractive stranger. Enjoy the moment. She'll probably be leaving soon, and you'll never see her again.

The waiter burst his daydream.

"Something from the kitchen?" he asked.

"Would you like to try the octopus?" Chris asked Erika. "Looks like he's about ready to take some off the grill."

"Why not," she replied. "Like they say, 'When in Rome...'" she smiled, raising her glass again.

Chris raised his glass to meet hers and they clinked a toast.

"*Oktophi mezethes*," Chris said to the waiter. "And two more ouzos, please." The waiter smiled and again disappeared.

"Careful, now," she said. "This is my first venture into these waters. I hear this stuff is pretty potent."

"Just something to sip on while we watch the sun go down. I can't handle much of it anyway. The Greeks say it's great for the digestion."

The sun was just about to touch the horizon. Without a cloud in the sky, the giant ball remained a fiery orange circle as it slipped further into the sea. They watched in silence as it finally disappeared, leaving a soft orange glow in the sky.

"I never get tired of seeing that," he said, "whether it's from the village or anywhere else in the world."

"Where is this fabled village," she asked.

"It's hanging off a cliff south of here in the mountains. But it's anything but fabled. A tiny little place called Stavroula."

"And you still have family there?"

"Sure do. Two older sisters, assorted aunts and uncles, and a string of cousins. My family immigrated to the U.S. during the Greek Civil War in 1948. My sisters were born in Greece, and I came along after we arrived in the States."

"So that's why you don't have an accent."

"Just the Alabama drawl, ma'am," he quipped.

The comment brought the first real smile that Chris had noticed across Erika's face. Her eyes seemed to sparkle as her lips parted, revealing a string of white teeth made even brighter when highlighted by her sun-dappled face. Two tiny dimples across each cheek completed the picture. Chris felt his heart pick up the pace again as their eyes met.

"You definitely should do that more often," he said.

"What's that?" Erika asked.

"Flash that devastating smile, of course."

"Now don't start with the Southern charm," she chided. "Combined with the 'Greek boy going home' routine, it might be just a little too much."

They both laughed and gazed out across the bay. A purple twilight was drenching the horizon as a few screeching seagulls were returning to their nests in the rocky cliffs. The temperature had dropped noticeably a few degrees, and the slight breeze drifting in from the ocean was refreshingly balmy after the heat of the day.

The waiter reappeared with a large platter containing a mound of octopus cut in small chunks garnished with several wedges of lemon. The octopus had just been taken off the grill and was still sizzling. The aroma was delightful, a tantalizing blend of smells that awakened the senses. There was a hint of charcoal and grilled fresh fish. Chris dutifully outlined for her the routine of squeezing the lemon over the meat and shaking a little oregano over the entire platter. Content that all was now in order, he speared a piece of octopus with his fork and offered it to her.

"The Greeks say '*Kali orexe*'," he said.

"Whatever," she said, taking the fork and nibbling at the meat. He watched as her eyes opened wide as she chewed.

"I like it! It's really quite good," she said excitedly. "I can't believe I'm eating it, but it really is very good. Not at all what I had imagined."

Chris asked the waiter for more lemons, a basket of bread, some feta cheese and black olives, and a dish of olive oil. When it arrived he again squeezed the lemons over the octopus and broke off a piece of the fresh baked bread to dunk in the olive oil. Erika followed his lead and was soon moving enthusiastically among all the items on the table. It wasn't long before they had emptied all the plates.

"The Greeks usually sit and talk now until later on in the evening when they have dinner," he said.

"Dinner?" she asked, slightly startled. "Good Lord, I couldn't eat anything else tonight. This was all the dinner I need. And it was excellent, really."

"How about some Greek coffee, then?"

"That I have been exposed to and, yes, I wou

Raising his hand for the waiter's attention, C
Greek coffees. The young boy returned with ‍
the thick, dark beverage and placed them on
pushed one in front of Erika and, as she reached for the cup, he
noticed for the first time that she was not wearing a ring on her
left hand. Could it be that she's not married? Maybe she's just left
the ring in her hotel in Athens. Steady again, boy. You're going
too fast. Slow down.

"How much of Greece are you planning to see?" he asked.

"I don't really have a set plan," she replied. "I have about ten
days. I'd like to do some of the sights on the mainland and spend
a couple of days in the islands. Not on a cruise, though. Maybe
just take one of the ferry boats. I've heard that Mykonos and
Hydra are very nice. Any suggestions?"

"Are you married?" he heard himself blurt out.

Her eyes opened wide behind the raised coffee cup. She
looked directly into his eyes and lowered the cup back to its
saucer. Pushing it away, she leaned back in her chair.

"Is this the going price for dinner?" she asked. "Now I'm
expected to waltz away with you?"

"No, no, no!" he stammered. "I'm really sorry. I didn't mean
to imply anything. Honestly. I was just going to suggest
something and I wouldn't feel right if you were married."

"You're digging the hole deeper."

"What I mean is I was going to propose something."

"Deeper still!"

He had been entertaining the notion and dreaming about what
she might say. The timing could have been better, but who knows
when and if the opportunity would arise again. Might as well just
show the cards right now.

"Listen to me. Let me finish before you say yes or no. I want
to invite you to go with me for a few days to my village for the
wedding. I know that sounds kind of hokey, but I honestly think
you would enjoy it. You'll get a glimpse of the real Greece, not
the tourist hotels and ritual sightseeing. The area is spectacular as
far as scenery goes and the wedding is going to be a lot of fun.

d be staying in my sister's house, and you'd have your own
oom. No strings attached. And I promise you will never lack for
chaperones, what with all the cousins, nieces, nephews, aunts, and
uncles around. There's a hydrofoil that leaves from the port in
Piraeus and takes us to a town called Leonidion, where we take a
taxi up into the mountains to Stavroula. The village has been
there since the Middle Ages and is home to only about 200 people
now. No hotel or restaurant, just a couple of coffee houses where
everyone congregates in the evening. Most of the young people
have left for jobs in Athens or the other big cities. They go back to
visit the old folks and to escape the heat in the summertime. The
hydrofoil runs daily to and from Athens. If you get bored,
uncomfortable, or decide it's not for you, I'll take you back to
Leonidion, get you a ticket on the hydrofoil, and we'll shake
hands and part as friends. You can't lose. What do you say?"

"I don't know you from Adam's house cat. I talk to you in a
bar…"

"*Taverna*," he interrupted, smiling. "Don't forget we're in
Greece."

"A *taverna*, then. Whatever. We meet, drink an ouzo, and I go
off with you to meet your family. We're visiting people I've never
met, staying in a place I've never seen, in a town I've never heard
of, in a country I've never visited. And I'm going with a man I
don't even know. You must think I…"

"The only thing I think is that I would love to show you some
of this country's most beautiful sights. Things the average tourist
never sees. I'd love for you to see the wedding, the village, and the
people."

"And if I was married you wouldn't extend the invitation?"

"Nope. I would feel uncomfortable in that situation."

"That's nice to know. How about you, are you married?"

"I've been divorced nine years. My wife finally grew tired of
the uncertainty of a writer's life. She had a very good job with the
telephone company. Regular paycheck, hours, office, benefits.
Everything I didn't have. She's married to a doctor now, and we
are still good friends."

Now it was Erika's mind that was racing. He seemed like a
nice enough guy. Attractive, fit, interesting to talk to. He knew

the language and the country. She could definitely see more of Greece with him than she would trying to find her way around alone. It might be fun. If she was uncomfortable she could leave. On the other hand, she had come here for the solitude and to try to forget. Did she want to be thrust into the middle of a strange family preparing for a wedding? What could there possibly be to do in a village of 200 people?

"The invitation sounds genuinely nice," she began.

Chris felt his heart sink. Oh well, it was a nice try.

"…but I just don't know."

His spirits suddenly lifted. She didn't actually say no!

"Listen," he suggested. "Think about it tonight. The hydrofoil leaves tomorrow at 10:00 a.m. from Piraeus and I'm leaving my hotel at about 8:30 for the pier. If you decide to chance it, come by and we'll cab together. If not, you go your way and I'll go mine. What do you say?"

She looked at him across the table. The impish twinkle had returned to his eye, and the grin still flashed across his face.

"When did you decide to ask me to go?" she asked.

"I thought about it when I first met you at the temple," he answered.

"Oh come on," she rolled her eyes. "Please spare me the…"

"I'm serious! I wear my feelings on my sleeve. I'm not going to lie to you. I thought you were incredibly attractive, and I daydreamed about going to the village together. I would love the company, and I really think you would enjoy the trip. I'm not eighteen years old, meaning I feel confident that I can keep my hormones in check. But I'm not going to sit here and beg. I've extended the offer, and I'll leave it with you."

"That's fair enough, and, seriously, I am flattered. Let me think about it tonight and I'll let you know in the morning. Is it a deal?"

"It is," Chris said. "Promise I won't mention it again. If you are going back to Athens I would appreciate a lift. If not I need to catch the bus."

"Guess I couldn't leave you to fight the crowds on the bus after all the free tourist information you gave me. Not to mention the incredible sunset and dinner."

Chris smiled and signaled for the waiter with the traditional writing gesture signifying he was ready for the bill. The waiter nodded and leafed through his notepad, totaling the charges. He placed the ticket on the table and waited as Chris counted out several bills and handed them to him.

"*Efharisto poli*," Chris said, thanking him.

The waiter nodded and returned the greeting. They rose to leave, and the old couple smiled at them. The old man said something to Chris in Greek, and he responded.

"Maybe I'll even pick up a little of the language while I'm here," Erika said.

"Depends on who your guide is," Chris smiled.

Chapter Two

The scrawny gray cat was peering cautiously at them from the edge of the parking lot as Chris and Erika left the taverna and headed for her car. The faint twilight would linger a while longer before the velvet curtain of the Mediterranean night completely descended, but most of the cars on the highway already had their headlights on. Erika opened the passenger door for Chris, and he crawled into the Toyota. He leaned across and lifted the latch of her door as she slid into the vehicle and tossed her purse into the back seat.

"I didn't even ask you if you wanted to drive," she said. "I'm sure you know the roads much better than I do."

"Thanks for not asking," he replied. "I hate driving in this city. It's a real free-for-all. Lanes mean nothing. Everybody just scrambles. About the only place I've seen that's worse is Cairo."

"You obviously haven't driven the Los Angeles freeway system lately."

It dawned on him just then that he did not know where she lived. The conversation had touched on a number of subjects, but he realized that he did not know where she was from.

"Is that your home?" he asked. "With all the interrogation I was doing at the *taverna*, I can't believe I overlooked that point."

"Newport Beach," she replied. "I was born in South Dakota, but my family moved to Southern California after I graduated from high school. I went to school at UCLA, and stayed in Los Angeles after I finished."

She pulled the Toyota into the traffic. It was still a little early for most of the day trippers to be returning to Athens, but there were already a number of cars and trucks jockeying for position on the four-lane road. As they drove past the beach resorts of Varkiza and Vouliagmeni, the tempo picked up, and by the time they reached the posh nightspots along Asteria Beach and Glyfada, the traffic was bumper to bumper.

The conversation centered mostly around how crowded the city had become and the urban sprawl which had engulfed Athens. Almost half of the country's 10 million people now lived in the city and its sprawling suburbs. There were no longer any discernible corporate limits delineating the beachside communities along the main traffic artery into the city center. Just an endless string of stores, apartments, restaurants, hotels, coffee shops, and *tavernas* in the resort towns. And a constant stream of cars, taxicabs, and green and white buses frantically transporting their passengers to destinations along the busy thoroughfare.

After passing the turn-off for the old international Elliniko Airport, the signs for the downtown center became numerous, and Erika followed them into the heart of the city.

"I love Athens for a day or two," Chris began, "but it closes in on me after that. I really enjoy getting away from all the traffic, noise, and congestion and escaping to the village."

He regretted the statement almost as soon as he had made it. That's enough of that, he thought. I'm running this village thing into the ground. She just told me she was from the big city. She's accustomed to the fast lane. Feels at home there. Now she probably thinks I'm still the hick from Small Town, Alabama who feels overwhelmed in the city.

Chris noticed how deftly she managed maneuvering through the lanes and stop-and-go pace of the clogged roadway. She even seemed impervious to the antics of the local kamikazes, the death defying maniacs on the big motorcycles and overloaded little scooters who were continually weaving in and out of traffic without regard to the huge trucks and buses that bore down on them. He was glad that he was not behind the wheel.

"Where are you staying in town?" she asked.

"I'm in a little hotel just off Syntagma Square," he said. "How about you?"

"I'm at the Hilton," she replied.

"That's near the American embassy," Chris said, "just up the road from me. You can just drop me at your hotel if you like. It's only a short cab ride or a twenty-minute walk to Syntagma. It will keep you out of the traffic jams in the square. They are still working on the underground subway station there and the streets are a mess."

"Are you sure?" she asked. "I was down there yesterday morning watching the changing of the guard at the unknown soldier's tomb in front of the Parliament building, and it seemed like a long way."

"No, really, it's fine. I can get a cab from the Hilton or walk off some of our dinner. I like walking in Athens, anyway. It seems like everywhere you look there is something out of a history book, and I love the people watching. The Greeks are so animated."

Erika laughed. She thought he was describing himself exactly. He gestured with his hands continually as he spoke and laughed with his eyes. He seemed to be constantly looking around, afraid that he might be missing something happening on another stage. Even though he appeared to be the typical laid back Southerner, he spoke enthusiastically about whatever the subject under discussion was.

"Greeks and Italians amaze me," she said. "If your hands were tied you people could not speak."

"It must be genetic," Chris said. "Watch the Greeks talking in a restaurant or coffee shop. They're waving their hands and making all kinds of gestures to get a point across. Just like an old sergeant I had in the army."

Her expression suddenly went blank. "You served in the army?" she asked, looking straight ahead. "When?"

"About 100 years ago," he said. "Draft board told me I was going to be all I could be."

She was silent for a moment. "Where did you go?" she asked.

"Where everybody went in the 60s," Chris said. "Vietnam, Republic of. The Asian Vacation. Recruiter told me I'd be making the world safe for democracy."

Erika's face lost all expression, and her gaze was riveted straight ahead. Even her hands seemed to tighten their grip on the steering wheel. Chris recognized the silence and looked at her. "Did I say something wrong?" he asked.

"No," she answered.

"I'm sorry if I touched a nerve or…"

"I said no," she snapped. "Please, just drop it."

The same far away look that gripped her at the temple at Sounion seemed to return. She was suddenly in another place. Her profile was as impassive as one on a coin. What was it that triggered these responses? He tried to remember what they were talking about at the temple that caused her to become so distant. No luck. Too many things on his mind. She had mentioned something about some time to herself. Trying to forget something, was that it?

They drove on in silence for what seemed like an eternity. He stared blankly at the automobile dealerships and repair shops along busy Sygrou Avenue as they came closer to downtown Athens. It seemed that each and every one of the high-rise apartment buildings had emptied its human contents into the restaurants and cafés along the broad avenue. All were jammed with people eating, talking, and reading newspapers. Even though they were still a few minutes from the heart of town, the floodlit Parthenon sitting atop the Acropolis hill came into view on their left. With lights strategically placed throughout the ruins, the ancient temple, dedicated to the virgin goddess who bestowed her name on the city, seemed to float in the night sky. Even the ravages of time and man during the temple's twenty-five-century existence had not dimmed the magnificence of this most perfect symbol of Greece. It was almost time for the nightly sound and light show to begin dazzling the crowds on the adjacent Philopappou Hill. The story of the city was told each evening in a memorable performance that included music, light, and a stirring narrative. Chris could imagine the crowds sitting in folding chairs beginning to zip up their jackets as the surprising cool of the spring evening replaced the heat of the day. He had returned to Greece a number of times with friends, and each time had made a point of taking them to the sound and light. He was wishing he could be there tonight with Erika, when she suddenly broke the silence.

"Do I stay on this street?" she asked.

"Just for a while longer," he said. "Up ahead the road forks when we reach the Temple of Olympian Zeus. If you bear to the right we can get on Konstantinou Street, which will take us right in front of the Hilton without having to go through Syntagma."

"That's quite a sight," she said, glancing to her left at the Acropolis.

"Nothing like it in the world," he said. "Have you been up there yet?"

"I went yesterday," she replied. "Really enjoyed it."

He didn't press the conversation further, as the silence once again overtook her. As they approached the ruins of the Temple of Olympian Zeus where the street divided, Chris recalled the first time his father had taken him to visit the site. He remembered feeling overwhelmed looking up at the sixteen Ionic and Corinthian columns, which were all that remained of the edifice that Aristotle proclaimed to be in the same class as the pyramids of Egypt. His father had detailed for him the construction of the temple that exceeded in magnitude all of the other temples of Greece and took over 700 years to complete. He thought it was strange that the edifice should have been consecrated by Hadrian, a Roman emperor, long after the golden age of Greece had passed. This had always been a special place for Chris, not only for the pride he felt at the accomplishments of his countrymen, but also for the memories it triggered of his father with whom he had been very close.

Erika turned right at the intersection and continued on Konstantinou Street past the Olympic Stadium, where the modern games were reintroduced to the world in 1896. It was not long before she was turning into the vehicle entrance to the Hilton Hotel.

A smartly uniformed parking valet opened the door for Erika and handed her a numbered ticket for her Toyota. She reached behind the driver's seat and retrieved her purse and travel bag. Chris was wrestling his own backpack out of the rear seat and looking around the interior to make sure he had not forgotten anything. He then went around the front of the car and handed the valet a few drachma notes. The young man tipped his hat and thanked him. Erika was standing on the top step in front of the door held open for them by another starched and spit-shined hotel employee. Inside, the lobby glistened with polished brass, marble, and a massive chandelier.

"Thank you for a lovely afternoon and evening," she said

smiling. "I really enjoyed it."

"Thank you for the great company," Chris said.

"How about a nightcap at the bar?" she asked. "My treat this time."

He looked at her for a long moment. Gazing into those incredible big blues, he felt his heart quicken again. She now seemed as cheerful and upbeat as she had been at the *taverna*, without a trace of the somber mood that had overtaken her on the ride into town.

"I'd better not," he said. "I'm still clearing a few of the cobwebs from the jet lag of yesterday's flight. I think I'll just stroll back to the hotel and crash."

Taking a pen and piece of paper from the outside pocket of his backpack, he scribbled something and gave it to her.

"This is the address of my hotel. It's the Hermes just two blocks from Syntagma. If you decide to take me up on the trip to the village, leave your car here at the hotel and give this to a cab driver. He won't have any trouble finding the hotel. I will be leaving around 8:30 in the morning."

She took the paper and looked at it. "Thank you," she said.

Standing in front of the hotel, with the breeze brushing her hair and her travel bag slung over her shoulder, she looked as stunning to him as when he had photographed her in front of the temple. A steady stream of guests ranging from pin-striped, buttoned-down business types to Arabs in flowing white robes and headdresses were entering and leaving the hotel, but Chris never noticed them. His gaze was fixed on Erika.

"I hope you'll decide to go," he said. "I would really like to see you again."

"I'll let you know," she said. To his astonishment, she hugged him and gave him a peck on the cheek. "You Greeks never shake hands," she smiled. "Everyone is always kissing. Thanks again for a great day."

Still in a mild state of shock, he watched her turn and walk into the hotel. Despite the throngs of after-five attired men and women in the lobby, Chris noticed how many heads were turning as Erika crossed the foyer in her simple sports clothes. He obviously was not the only one taken by her. He watched until she vanished behind a line of giant marble columns in front of the elevators.

Chris looked at the smiling doorman who was standing in a parade-rest position, his gloved hands behind his back, next to the revolving door. "Very beautiful, the lady," the doorman said.

"Yes," Chris agreed, "she definitely is that."

Chris walked across the hotel driveway and onto the sidewalk. Shouldering his pack, his hands in his pockets, he began walking back to his hotel, oblivious to the noisy stream of traffic rattling along Vasilissis Sofias Street, also known as "millionaires' row". The night air was cool and pleasant despite being warmed by buses, trucks, and cars belching smoke and diesel fumes. It was somewhat ironic that these symbols of modern civilization were quickly accomplishing what time and a host of invaders and conquerors had been unable to do. The marble of the ancient temples and monuments had been harmed more in the last four decades by the sulphuric acid in the polluted air than from all the damage wrought on them during the previous two and a half millennia.

Chris hardly noticed the various museums and brass signs on the exterior walls of the buildings that housed the many foreign embassies located along the wide boulevard. Some were huge, elaborate villas with gardens, guards, and scores of employees, while others, housing the diplomats of tiny African or Southeast Asian nations, were modest structures hardly larger than some of the grand homes in the neighborhood.

Walking towards Syntagma Square, he could see the lights of the Parthenon shimmering above the city on the Acropolis hill in the distance, an eternal reminder to Athenians and the city's visitors that Western civilization had begun here over 2,000 years before. Of all the voices over the ages that had glorified the city in praise and prose, Chris's father felt that John Milton's encapsulation of Athens in *Paradise Regained* stood as the ultimate sketch of the city. "Athens, the eye of Greece," Milton wrote, "mother of arts and eloquence, the olive grove of Academe, Plato's retirement, where the Attic bird trills her thick-warbled notes the summer long." No one could top that.

Dodging the raucous, horn-blowing drivers as he crossed the

streets, the same familiar sadness descended over him as it did each time he returned to Athens to see what had happened to the city. This first great European metropolis of the ancient world was now suffering from ailments common to cities almost everywhere—overcrowding, pollution, and horrendous traffic. Chris enjoyed his brief visits here, but he was always anxious to return to Stavroula. Despite Athens's ageless monuments to the glory of Greece, the village was where he felt his strongest ties to the country of his parents. It kept him connected with his family and his past. While growing up in the United States, he had returned many times to Greece with his parents, and had spent much time with his sisters and relatives in the village. His roots went deep into the rocky soil there, and no place he had ever visited in his travels around the world had ever woven a spell so complete on him.

He found his pace quickening as he approached the busy square in front of the Parliament building. He stopped to pick up a copy of the *International Herald Tribune*, a Snickers bar, and a lemon soda at a kiosk at the far end of the square. The two short blocks from there to the Hermes Hotel brought him into the fringe of the Plaka area, the old quarter of the city on the lower slopes of the Acropolis hill.

Chris entered the small lobby of the Hermes, thinking how it contrasted with the posh luxury of the Hilton. A small tourist property, the Hermes was popular with young Europeans and backpackers who wanted a basic room at a cheap price. He stayed a night or two there on each of his visits to Greece, and the hotel staff knew him by name. There were no amenities like the swimming pools, business offices, upscale restaurants, and night clubs of the big international hotels. The lobby had two tired old sofas and a few chairs, where a handful of college students were poring over a series of maps outlining their travel plans. A young man was absorbed in a magazine he was reading behind the small bar located near the tiny elevator. A wall rack held a half-dozen bottles of Campari, Black Label Johnny Walker Scotch, Canadian Club, and assorted other liquors coated with a film of dust, that attested to their recent inactivity. He picked up his key from a smiling night manager at the front desk, and walked up the two flights of stairs to his room.

He had left the windows closed when he departed the hotel earlier that afternoon, and the room was uncomfortably warm despite the relative cool of the evening. The hotel boasted air conditioning, but even on the maximum setting the ancient apparatus barely eked out enough cool air to make the small room comfortable. Chris wondered how stifling it must be there in July.

Crossing the room to the door opening onto his tiny balcony, he walked out and looked down at the people shuffling along narrow Apollonos Street two floors beneath him. His room faced south and, had he been on an upper floor, he would have had a wonderful view of the Acropolis just a half-dozen blocks away. As it was, however, he was content to contemplate the ancient buildings from the hotel's tiny rooftop bar that he sometimes visited in the late afternoon. Closer to the base of the Acropolis were the teeming crowds and late night *tavernas* and tourist shops that never seemed to close. Even at this distance, he could hear bouzouki tunes drifting from the outdoor restaurants and shops in the Plaka. He sat on the plastic lawn chair on his balcony and, propping his feet on the wrought iron railing, sipped his lemon soda and savored the Snickers bar. Surely two of life's great pleasures, he thought.

Try as he might to focus on other things, his thoughts kept returning to Erika. He could not remember the last time he had been so completely captivated by a woman, especially in so brief a period of time. He had dated numerous women since his divorce, and he went out pretty regularly when he was at home. There had even been what he considered to be serious relationships. Since his divorce from Carolyn, however, almost nine years ago, he had never really totally committed himself to one woman. And here I am now, he thought, getting cross-eyed over a woman I'll probably never see again.

Finishing his soda and candy bar, he went back inside the room and returned the few clothes he had unpacked to the depths of his duffel bag. The remaining shaving items and magazines would go into his backpack in the morning when he was ready to check out. After a quick shower, he stretched out on the room's single bed with his hands clasped behind his head and stared at the ceiling.

Would she call? Would she show up in the morning? What was it he said that had tripped her mood swings? Was it actually something he said or just a shadow that periodically crept over her? He recounted the events of the day over and over for a clue.

Could it have been the reference to the military? Was it Vietnam? She became silent and pensive after that and never really came out of it until they arrived at her hotel. Had someone in her family served in the military during that time? Had she lost a friend or relative during those years? Did she resent his off-the-cuff remarks about the army?

Chris wrestled with his thoughts long after the moon had finally set in the night sky. When sleep finally overtook him, he was once again a scared nineteen-year-old rifleman in an infantry platoon slogging through a rice field in Vietnam's Iron Triangle.

Chapter Three

The sound of a door closing down the hall eased Chris from a deep sleep into a state of semi-consciousness. With his eyes still closed, he rolled over in bed and drew his pillow tightly to his chest. Suddenly, he snapped into an awakened state and looked at the travel alarm clock on his night stand. 6:35. Plenty of time. It would be another half-hour before the alarm would go off. Relaxing back in bed, he stared for a few moments at the ceiling.

Well, he thought, she didn't call. Guess she's not coming after all. A deep breath and long sigh punctuated his disappointment. Wait a minute! Check with the front desk, he thought. Maybe she phoned and they didn't ring my room. His excitement returned. Sitting up in bed, he dialed reception and inquired as to whether there had been any phone calls or messages. Sorry, there had been none. Oh well, he yawned. Life goes on.

Chris returned the phone to its receiver and extended his arms towards the ceiling in the long, reaching stretch of a cat waking from a long nap. Still in his jockey shorts, he walked out on his balcony and looked down at the closed shutters and padlocked roll-down doors of the shops in the deserted street below. As it was a Saturday, the few small business offices in the area would not be opening, and it was too early for the tourist shops to roll up their doors and begin welcoming the legions of gawking visitors who would be strolling through the area on their way to and from the Acropolis. The coffee houses and bakeries scattered through the neighborhood evidenced the only signs of life, as their owners scurried around inside, preparing for the routine visits of the Greeks who lived in the old district. They came almost daily for their morning jolt of the strong Greek coffee and a fresh baked roll or pastry while they swapped gossip and their analyses of life in general. It was a scene that had repeated itself in the Plaka and throughout Greece for over two millennia. The tiny *kafenion* had always been the center of life in Greece and now, even in the days of CNN and satellite news coverage, the institution still retained its undisputed role as the primary forum from which the Greeks expounded their views on everything from politics to the weather. Chris liked to imagine this same scene 2,500 years ago, when most of the city's residents lived here in the shadow of the Acropolis. What would Plato or Socrates have discussed while lounging with friends over a decanter of wine in the shade of an awning near this very spot? He envied their good fortune at having been spared the omnipresent pollution and incessant noise that was now an accepted part of life in Athens. The current denizens of the city went about their daily business seemingly oblivious to the cacophony of horns from automobiles, trucks and buses weaving through the city's clogged arteries and the din of construction underway almost everywhere. He contrasted that with the overwhelming quiet of Stavroula. The only sounds he remembered there were the wind caressing the acacia and cedar trees on the mountain and the tinkling of bells around the necks of the goats which were constantly on the move, foraging for food in the hard scrabble hills.

He was suddenly conscious of the cool morning, and went back inside and closed the balcony door. Switching on the light in the tiny bathroom, he looked at himself in the mirror. His eyes appeared somewhat tired. Not much sleep last night, he thought. Still a little jet lag too. It usually took a couple of days for his body to adapt to the local time, whether he was on holiday here in Greece or on writing assignments in Africa, Asia, or any of the other nooks and crannies of the world where his work had carried him.

Suddenly, the phone was ringing. Chris's heart began racing. He ran to the bedside and picked up the handset.

"Hello," he said nervously.

For a moment there was silence. "Sorry, I have wrong number," a man said in broken English on the other end.

Chris put the phone down and felt the air again go out of his sails. Probably one of the hotel guests, he thought. Sounded German.

"I've got to get over this," Chris said out loud. "She decided not to come and that's that. It was a pleasant afternoon. Just that and nothing more. Get over it."

Still, he could not help picturing her in his mind silhouetted against the Temple of Poseidon with the sun setting behind her on the horizon. Her playful enthusiasm, experimenting with the octopus and ouzo in the *taverna*. The breeze rustling her hair. The rosy sun glow on her face. And her eyes. The incredible, piercing blue of her eyes. She's going to take some getting over, he thought. He was still amazed at how smitten he had become during the brief encounter.

Chris shaved and stepped into the shower stall. Adjusting the hot and cold water handles to a slightly more than warm temperature, he began showering with the long, hand-held contraption that he had never been able to get accustomed to using. Spray yourself from head to toe. Soap up. Rinse. It was like the cycles in a washing machine. One of the things he missed most about home when he was on the road was the standard American shower. Most European hotels and homes still clung to the hand-held shower technology. Guess ours use too much water, he thought. Everything to excess in America.

From his duffel bag he retrieved a white T-shirt, and enjoyed its crisp, clean feel as he pulled it over his head. He stepped into the jeans he had laid out last night and laced up his tennis shoes. Walking over to the dresser, he slipped the chain with the Saint Christopher pendant over his head. He stared at the faded figure of the saint carrying a small child on his shoulders and thought back to the day so long ago when his mother had placed it in his hand. The patron saint of travelers, Saint Christopher had greater status in the Roman Catholic Church than in Chris's own Greek Orthodox religion, but his mother was a big fan of the man anyway. She even named Chris after him. Fresh from a single year of college, Chris had been waiting on the Greyhound bus that would carry him from Mobile, Alabama to the Army Reception Center at Fort Benning, Georgia, when his mother had given him the medallion. With tears in her eyes, she had kissed him and told him to wear it always wherever he went and Saint Christopher would protect him. His father had pressed a twenty-dollar bill into his hand and wrapped him in a huge bear hug. The money was still a tidy sum for an eighteen-year-old in 1968. Chris wondered what his father probably had to do without that week to be able to slip him the money. The small wholesale produce company his dad operated had afforded the family a decent living, but was steadily being squeezed out of existence by the giant food suppliers and the mega-stores.

The saint had definitely worked overtime keeping an eye on Chris. His twelve-month tour of duty in Vietnam had been spent mostly in the bush. Assigned to a mechanized infantry brigade in the 25th Infantry Division, headquartered in Cu Chi, he had seen almost continuous action while in the country. Everything from search and destroy missions to closing off escape routes for North Vietnamese units slipping back and forth across an unseen border with Cambodia.

Chris thought it was strange that his dreams the previous night had been invaded by the familiar faces that had haunted his sleep for several years after his return from Southeast Asia. Like most returning veterans, he had attended psychotherapy sessions conducted by post traumatic stress disorder specialists who attempted to exorcise the demons and heal the emotional scars of combat which plagued a generation of young men who had grown old overnight in the jungle. Some never completely recovered nor learned to adjust to a world that knew little and cared even less about what they had experienced.

Time is a great healer, however, and the year that Chris spent in that special corner of hell was like another world to him now. His sleep was rarely troubled by those events of over three decades ago. He returned the necklace inside his T-shirt and, picking up his room key, went downstairs to breakfast.

The Hermes included, as was the custom in most European-style hotels in Athens, continental breakfast daily with the price of the room. The room in which breakfast was served was on the first floor. "One level up from the ground floor," the desk clerk had reminded him. "Don't forget, here in Greece is different," he smiled.

Few other guests were up and moving about this early on Saturday morning. Two tall blonde women were seated at a table near the room's far wall. Their bulging backpacks were leaning against the table, and they were examining a map as they ate.

Chris walked along the buffet table and selected a package of Corn Flakes from the few cereal items available. There was also a platter of cheese and assorted cold cuts which he bypassed, a bowl of hard-boiled eggs, and a weathered cutting board with a huge, round loaf of bread. Chris picked up one of the eggs, a couple of scoops of marmalade, and sliced off a large chunk of the bread. He carried everything to his table and returned for a glass of juice.

Two other guests entered the room and walked to the buffet table to browse the options.

"Room number please?" a young girl asked, approaching Chris's table.

"Two-one-three," he replied, placing his room key next to his juice.

She wrote his room number down on her pad. "Coffee?" she asked, smiling.

"Yes, please," he said.

Watching the girl pour his coffee, Chris thought she fit the stereotypical image of the Mediterranean woman exactly. Dark eyes, a narrow face, and long brown hair that she had pulled back with a white ribbon. Chris wondered if the old custom of single women wearing a white ribbon in their hair to signify their availability for marriage was still part of Greek life. He doubted it. So much had changed in recent years, not only in the big cities but in the countryside as well. Many of the villagers still clung to the old customs and traditions, but the Greeks in general prided themselves on their cosmopolitan lifestyle and acceptance of all things modern. There was now a McDonald's with the latest Disney collectible cartoon characters in the heart of Syntagma Square, and all the local youngsters had learned to wear their baseball caps backwards. All the accoutrements of our present civilization in the cradle of ancient civilization.

The waitress refilled Chris's coffee cup, and he thanked her. Looking at his watch, he saw that it was almost eight o'clock. He would call a taxi in about a half-hour to take him to the port of Piraeus where he would board the ten o'clock hydrofoil for the trip to Leonidion and on to Stavroula. A great many Greeks as well as tourists were now relying on the speedy hydrofoils to zip them to the picture postcard islands and to port cities clinging to

37

the miles of rocky shoreline on Greece's indented coast. The ferry boats were cheaper, but the hydrofoils cut the travel time drastically. The enclosed cabins with assigned seating in airline-style reclining chairs also offered a much more pleasant journey, especially if the ocean was kicking up at all. He should arrive in Leonidion around 12:30, where he would hire a taxi to carry him up the five-mile mountain road to his village.

Chris had phoned Maria, his older sister, from Kennedy Airport before he left and told her he would be arriving sometime Saturday. He smiled, knowing she would have a big meal still warm on the stove awaiting his arrival.

Chris finished his breakfast, and left a few drachmas on the table for the service. As he was leaving, the young girl walked up to him and thanked him for the gratuity. Most of the young backpackers who stayed at the hotel were not in the habit of leaving tips, and the waitress was very appreciative.

Returning to his room, Chris brushed his teeth and tied a red bandana around his head. His hair did not come down below his collar, but he knew it would be windy later on in the day, especially at the port. He would clip his baseball cap to his backpack and not worry about it blowing away.

Chris tucked his shaving kit along with his magazines and travel alarm into his backpack and zipped it shut. Looking around the room one last time, he hoisted his duffel bag over one shoulder and his backpack over the other and eased out the door, pulling it shut behind him. He walked down the hall to the elevator and pressed the call button. His load was not too heavy, but he chose to ride rather than walk down the two flights of stairs.

When it arrived, Chris turned sideways to enter the tiny elevator, and pressed the button for the lobby. He thought how impossible it would be for the conveyance to carry more than two people even without baggage. It groaned and creaked its slow journey to the lobby level, and Chris was glad to exit the aging contraption when it finally stopped.

The only people in the lobby were two cleaning women in blue uniform dresses and blue scarves on their heads, dragging their cleaning equipment out of a closet. Chris walked to the reception desk, where a smiling attendant instantly appeared from a rear office.

"You enjoyed your stay, Mr. Chris?" he asked.

"It was very nice, George," Chris answered. "I'll be in the village for about eight days and will be back here next Tuesday for one night."

"We have you reserved for one night," the clerk said.

"Sounds great," said Chris.

"You leave the charges on your credit card?"

"Yes, please."

The clerk slid the completed account statement across the counter for Chris to review.

"Looks fine," he said, signing the charge. "See you next week."

"Have a good trip," the clerk smiled.

Chris carried his bags to the entrance, where he placed them in a chair next to the door. He walked outside and looked up and down Apollonos Street. Private cars were parked with one wheel on the sidewalk on both sides of the narrow, one-way street, leaving a route down the middle of the thoroughfare where a single vehicle could barely pass. There were a couple of taxis in front of the Apollo Hotel, a larger property a half block up the street, but no room for a cab stand in front of the Hermes. He would get his gear and hail one of the cabs from the front of the Apollo.

Chris went back inside to retrieve his bags and make sure everything was zipped up tight. He waved goodbye to the clerk, walked out to the curb, and placed his bags next to a large flower pot with a dwarf Norfolk pine growing in it.

"Is the invitation still open?" a voice asked.

Chris looked up and was stunned. In front of him was the familiar white Toyota with Erika behind the steering wheel flashing her disarming smile behind a pair of Ray Ban sunglasses. She wore a long billed baseball cap with her hair pulled back in a ponytail underneath it. A white Nautica jacket with the sleeves pushed up covered a pink boat-neck T-shirt.

"I don't believe it," he said, walking out into the street to the car.

She removed her sunglasses and looked up at him. The face

with the piercing blue eyes was exactly how he had remembered it.

"I thought about it last night," she began, "and decided that 'what the heck', I don't have much time in Greece, and I'm sure I'll see much more of the country with you than I would on my own. You seem like a nice enough guy, and I'm a big girl. Learned to take care of myself a long time ago. I've never been to a Greek wedding, but I've heard they are a lot of fun. And it sounds like no trip to Greece would be complete without seeing this village you keep talking about. So here I am."

Chris was beaming. "That's great," he said. "You decided to bring your car?"

"Maybe it's my safety net," she smiled. "I figure we can drive there and have a car to get around with. And if the whole thing is too much for me I can bail. Is it a deal?"

"You bet," Chris said. "The drive takes longer than the hydrofoil, but it's a good road and we'll pass through some beautiful country. We're in no rush to get there so we can stop for a picnic along the way if you like."

"Sounds great, let's get going," she said, flipping him the car keys. Chris opened her door and she swung her long legs out of the car. She put her sunglasses back on, removed her jacket, and tossed it into the back seat.

"Do you want to put your bags in the trunk?" she asked. "I've got a lot of junk in the back seat."

"Sure," he said. He opened the trunk of the Toyota and whistled. "Wow!" he exclaimed. "Looks like a lot back here too."

"Now don't start with the packing jokes," she smiled. "I didn't know how much to bring, what I needed to wear to the wedding, and what I should leave at the Hilton for when I return, so I just brought it all. Is there room?"

"No problem. I can get my bag back here and I'll put the backpack in the back seat."

"Is that all you have?"

"I keep some clothes at my sister's house in the village," he replied. "That way I don't have to carry a lot of stuff when I visit. Sweaters for colder weather, a jacket for church, hiking boots, that kind of stuff. Makes it easy."

"Do you mind driving? I don't have a clue where we're going."

"All part of my plan," Chris said smiling. "Keep her totally in the dark as to where we are and where we're going. The whole works."

She rolled her eyes. "I can tell this is going to be an interesting few days."

Chris laughed as he opened the passenger door for Erika. She slid in and pulled down the visor to check the position of her hat and sunglasses in the mirror. Satisfied that both were in order, she buckled her seatbelt.

Chris got in and immediately slid the seat back to accommodate his longer legs. Adjusting the rear-view mirror and the outside mirrors, he put the Toyota in gear and headed down the street into the heart of the Plaka.

Chapter Four

On a weekday, Apollonos Street and the narrow alleyways feeding it would be jammed with an endless stream of pedestrians and horn-blowing cars and trucks, but on a Saturday morning it was next to deserted. Chris cruised down the ancient cobblestoned thoroughfare until they reached the church of Ayios Eleftheros. A handful of men were sweeping down the entranceways to the coffee shops and restaurants that lined the plaza. Some of the shops were already open for business and had newspaper readers and coffee drinkers enjoying the balmy morning at tables set under the tall eucalyptus trees. Passing the church, Chris picked up Pandrossou Street which led to Monasteraki. This was the heart of the Plaka, and vendors would later occupy almost every square inch of street and sidewalk. Monasteraki was Athens's most famous flea market. The underground train station was a magnet drawing villagers eager to sell everything from hand-woven rugs to old automobile parts, copper pots, or used clothing. Looking at the ruins spread over a large open space to her left, Erika asked, "What is all that?"

"That's the *agora*," Chris replied. "In ancient times it was the heart of the city. It was the center of daily life, where people shopped and swapped news and gossip. Their own little soap operas. Philosophers taught in the buildings that stood there, and the apostle Paul later used those rocks as his soap box to preach to the Athenians."

Chris turned right on Athinas Street, the major thoroughfare that would carry them to Omonia Square and the bedlam that, during the week, centered around the plaza over the underground railway station.

Traffic was still light, and it was not long before they were moving quickly westward along Athinas, which served as the main exit from Athens to the Peloponnese. The highway follows the Route of the Sacred Way, which in ancient times connected

Athens and the town of Eleusis.

Chris noticed Erika's wide-eyed enthusiasm at the sites along the way. She became especially animated as the highway climbed the rocky slopes of Mount Egaleo and passed the monastery of Daphni.

"That is incredible," she exclaimed as they drove past the monastery's high walls and battlements.

"It's almost 1,000 years old," Chris said. "Supposed to be one of the most important monasteries in Greece. There are dozens of mosaics and icons inside depicting the godliest saints and the worst sinners. If you are ever here in the summer there is a wonderful wine festival beginning in July which features food, music, dancing, and wine from all over Greece. Really a lot of fun."

"I guess it gives me an excuse to come back," she said coyly.

Chris felt his heart quicken again. He glanced at Erika. She was smiling and looking straight ahead.

Careful, he thought. She's just having some fun. It's just a passing comment. Don't read anything into it. God, he wondered, is my interest in her really that obvious?

His attention returned to the highway which, after Daphni, plunged to the Bay of Eleusis, the northern fringe of the Saronic Gulf. The area was scarred by refineries, shipyards, and the hulks of dozens of old freighters rusting away on their anchor chains in the bay. The island of Salamis lay gray and brooding in the distance. Chris pointed out the narrow straits where the Greeks destroyed the fleet of the Persian invaders in the fifth century before Christ in one of history's most crucial battles.

"If the Greeks had lost that one," he related, "the course of history would have been changed. Greek civilization, on which much of Western Civilization was built, would never have gotten off the ground."

"You are sounding like the guidebook again. You must have spent a lot of time studying Greek history."

"I'm sorry," he said. "I get started talking about all this and I just get carried away. Just tell me to shut up when I begin a dissertation."

"I'm just teasing. I've read basic history, but who remembers all this? Old for us in the States is 200 years. Here we're looking at more than 2,000 years of recorded time, and it really amazes me. I've always wanted to visit these sights, and I want to hear anything you can tell me about them."

"Only if you will tell me more about yourself."

"Depends on what you want to know."

"As much as you're willing to tell."

"I guess that's fair enough. Like I told you yesterday, I was born in South Dakota and moved to the West Coast after high school. No sisters, but one older brother. My mother and father are divorced. Mom is a country club socialite living in Santa Monica and Dad is a retired computer wonk in Glendale. He made a lot of money designing micro-chips in the 70s and early 80s. I finished UCLA with a journalism degree, and have been working with magazines ever since. I became more interested in the photographic end of the industry and got an associate degree in photography. Have worked for *Western Woman* magazine for fourteen years."

"And no husband or babies?"

"There was a husband once," she said, "but no babies. My work keeps me pretty busy now."

Chris noticed that she seemed much more comfortable talking about herself now than she had been earlier, but she still only volunteered basic data. He made mental notes on the information she offered, and resolved not to delve further into her private life.

The highway on which they were traveling became part of the national toll road running north to Thessaloniki and south to Corinth and the Peloponnese. The route hugged the coast hemmed in by assorted factories and a few nondescript towns.

Even though it was mid-morning, the temperature had already climbed into the mid-70s. The sky, despite the heavy orange haze, was an impossible blue, without a cloud on the horizon. May in Greece was usually a predictable string of warm, sunny days and cool nights, and had become a favorite time for many tourists before the apocalyptic heat and throngs of vacationers closed in for the summer. It was also the most colorful season, with mountain wildflowers showing off their riotous colors before the parched, rain-free summer months scorched everything and coated the landscape with a blanket of dust.

The scenery was becoming more mountainous and the coastal belt was fringed with pine trees. The green contrasted sharply with the monochromatic barrenness of the rocks and reminded Chris that he was only a few hours away from the tall cedar trees standing sentinel over the stone houses and the small church in Stavroula.

"We'll be at the Corinth Canal soon," he said. "I thought you might want to stop for a cold drink and some photographs."

"Sounds great," she said. "Is there much to see?"

"Not really. The canal was dug about 100 years ago. It had been talked about in ancient times, and digging had even started on a few occasions. They used to drag their ships across the isthmus to save the long trip around the Peloponnese. There is a nice view as we cross the bridge there. The canal is only about seventy-five feet wide, and even the smaller cruise ships and ferry boats seem to be almost scraping the sides."

Erika reached into the back seat and dug her camera bag out of the pile of jackets and shopping bags there. She opened the bag, removed a Nikon and began examining the lenses. Loading a roll of sixty-four speed film into the Nikon, she took a sheet of tissue paper and rubbed it carefully over her lenses.

As they pulled off the main road into the maze of shops and restaurants on the eastern bank of the canal, Chris looked for the *souvlaki* shop where he usually stopped on his way south. The area was crowded with automobiles and campers heading out of town for the weekend. He parked the car next to a kiosk covered with magazines and newspapers, and turned off the engine.

"Better lock it up," he said. "You won't have to worry about the Greeks, but I can't say the same for all these tourists here."

They got out of the Toyota and walked onto the porch of a large white building with painted signs of shish kabobs, sandwiches, groceries, and drinks. A number of people were sipping drinks on the porch, and the door and all the windows were open.

"The restrooms are downstairs," Chris said. "I'll get us a table. Would you like something to drink?"

"Coke for me," she said. "I'll be back in a minute."

Chris took a seat at a round white table and glanced at the

plastic covered menu listing in Greek and English dozens of items which the restaurant never seemed to have available. The waiter approached and Chris ordered two Cokes. He watched the traffic on the busy highway and the huge crowds walking out onto the bridge for photographs. There must be a ship passing through, he thought.

Erika reappeared, smiling. She held a plastic bag with several items inside.

"What's funny?" he asked. "Were the restrooms okay?"

"Oh, they were fine," she said. "I just picked up a couple of items to take with us, and I'm not really sure what they are. They looked good, though."

She opened the bag and showed him a package of figs and a box of crackers.

"I take it these are dried figs," she said, holding up the fruit bound with a heavy string and wrapped in plastic.

"And they are very good," he said. "You cut the string and peel the figs off as you want them. They taste great and last forever. What else have you got?"

"Just some crackers and a couple of bottles of water," she said. "I'm always thirsty."

The waiter appeared with their drinks and Chris handed him several drachma notes. He opened the Cokes and poured them into the two glasses.

"To good company," Chris said, raising his glass.

"To good company," Erika echoed.

"Are you hungry," he asked. "We can order something if you feel like eating."

"Not really," she said. "I ate at the hotel before I left. I'd just as soon pick up something for that picnic you mentioned."

"Great," said Chris excitedly. "Would you like to take a look at the canal? From the looks of the crowd on the bridge, there must be a ship going through."

"Sure," Erika said. She returned her purchases to her bag, took a long drink from her Coke and put the glass on the table. They walked across the parking lot and joined the flow of pedestrians walking out on to the bridge spanning the canal.

"Oh look!" Erika exclaimed. "There is a ship transiting. I'm going back to the car to get my camera."

"Do you want me to get it?" he asked.

"No, you save our place here," she said pointing to the shoulder-to-shoulder crowd peering over the railing at the ship creeping slowly through the narrow waterway.

"You'll need these, then," he said tossing her the car keys.

"I'll be right back," she said. Erika turned and trotted across the parking lot to her car. Of the 100 or so people crowding the bridge, ninety-nine were observing the progress of the ship through the canal. Chris alone was looking the other way, watching Erika as she trotted across the parking lot. The ponytail swung to and fro as she moved. Her run was fluid and easy, like that of one accustomed to such movement. The stride was long and sure, and she held her arms parallel to the ground in the manner of a distance runner. Chris had always been attracted to athletic women, and this one appeared to be incredibly fit as well as beautiful.

I admit it, he thought. I am hooked.

He realized that Erika had totally captured his imagination, and he thought about how fortunate he was that she had decided to spend a few days traveling with him.

Chris was leaning against the railing with his back to the canal as Erika returned with her camera. She realized that he had been looking at her rather than at the approaching ship.

"Why the smile?" she asked.

"No reason," he said. "Just happy."

"Hold the smile, then, and let me get your picture." She snapped a couple of frames of Chris leaning back against the railing with the ship in the background.

He turned around as she stood next to him while the crowd on the bridge waved to the crew and passengers of the ship easing through the canal. The vessel was an older cruise liner, and her decks were crowded with oil-slathered sun worshippers lounging around the pools on the aft decks. She was small enough to slip through the canal into the Gulf of Corinth on her way to Patras and the Ionian Sea beyond. The larger, newer ships were far too large for the canal, and sailed from Piraeus around the Peloponnese on their itineraries to Italy and the western

Mediterranean. *waved* *leaned*

Erika was waving to the passengers and leaning forward as the ship passed directly beneath them. She placed her hand on Chris's arm as she stood on her tiptoes for a better view. It was obviously an unconscious move on her part, and she continued to follow the movement of the ship below the bridge. But to Chris the touch was electric. He felt his heart racing as her closeness further intoxicated him. Finally, she came down off her tiptoes and, picking up her camera bag, replaced the Nikon and zipped the bag shut.

"That was amazing," she said. "It looks like the ship is scraping the sides of the canal."

Chris felt his composure returning.

"It's quite a sight," he said. "I went through once on a ferry boat going to Corfu. It's as impressive looking up as it was just now looking down."

While most of the crowd remained on the bridge watching the ship, Chris and Erika turned away and began walking back to the car. He unlocked her door and held it open as she slid into the passenger's seat.

"Still the Southern gentleman, eh?" she smiled.

"Still trying," he answered.

Chris walked around to his side of the Toyota and stopped to buy a newspaper from a very large lady in the kiosk in the parking lot. When he got into the car he placed the paper on the console between their seats and buckled his seatbelt.

"I would think this language is incredibly difficult to learn," Erika said, opening the newspaper. "A different alphabet, accent marks, the whole thing."

"It is pretty different, but after you catch on to the letters it's not that bad. Actually, it's much more definite than English."

"How far are we from—how did you pronounce the name of your village?"

"Stavroula. It's about three hours from here. With a stop for lunch, a little longer."

Chris pulled the Toyota back onto the highway and rejoined the stream of traffic on the toll road. In a few minutes they arrived at the broad, eight-lane toll payment area. Only three booths in each direction were open and cars were lined up to pay the 500 drachmas toll.

"Do you need any local money?" Erika asked.

"No, no. I've got the exact amount right here," Chris said, taking the notes out of his wallet. He noted how the Greeks have not yet perfected the concept of exact change lanes or the automatic toll both, and that each station was manned by a bored-looking attendant in the ubiquitous blue shirt. Chris handed him the money and received a yellow ticket that he placed on the dash.

"You pay one price even though you may not be going the full distance on the highway," he said. "We'll be getting off in a few miles near the town of Corinth."

"That was a pretty famous place in ancient days, wasn't it? What's it like now?"

"A few restored ruins, but nothing spectacular. Its primary importance was from the apostle Paul's visits there. I thought we might stop for a look on the way back to Athens. There's a pretty nice picnic stop further down near Mycenae, and it's much more picturesque there."

"Sounds okay to me. You're the guide."

Erika eased back into her seat and lowered her window slightly.

"Would you like me to turn on the air?" Chris asked.

"No, I'm not that warm. Just thought I'd enjoy a little of the fresh air."

Chris cracked his window open also. The air was warm and dry and felt good on his skin.

"How about some tunes on the radio?" Erika asked, adjusting the dials. "Let's see what our options are." She began surfing the stations. Most were Greek music channels, with a few rock stations playing the music of European and American artists.

"What's your preference?" Chris asked.

"How about the Greek music? I like the bouzouki sound, and I love to watch the dancing."

"Great! You'll get a chance to see plenty of that at the wedding. Most of the village will turn out for the event. They'll have a band and tons of food and dancing."

"I have to tell you, I fell in love with the idea of Greece after I saw *Zorba the Greek*. I love the spirit of the Greeks, the culture and history, and especially Zorba's outlook on life. I thought the scene of Anthony Quinn dancing on the beach after his grand scheme collapsed was one of the most romantic things I've ever seen."

"That was a great movie," Chris said. "Anthony Quinn was the perfect person to play that role."

After a moment of silence, Erika turned to face Chris. "Will you teach me to dance?" she asked.

He was a little taken aback by the suddenness of her question, and the feeling must have shown on his face. He looked at her for a long second. Even with the hat and her hair in a ponytail the wind was scattering her hair across her face. She had removed her sunglasses and her eyes were looking directly into his. Chris felt she could see all the way into his soul. Her mood seemed playful and happy, but her question and the look in her eyes were very intense. Was there something else behind the question? Was this another of the roller coaster mood swings which seemed to regularly transform this woman?

"I'd love to," he said, his eyes returning finally to the road.

Chapter Five

Traffic was relatively light when Chris left the National Road at the exit indicating the route to Corinth and the southern Peloponnese. He turned again before entering the town of Corinth, taking the spur that would bypass the city. He explained to Erika how Corinth in antiquity had become the largest city and commercial center of Greece, but its wealth led to its pillaging and destruction by the Romans in the second century B.C. Except for a smattering of restorations of the ruins associated with Paul's letters to the Corinthians, little remained to entice the visitor today. The physical setting of the area is now its most notable feature.

Erika was awestruck with the imposing mass of Acrocorinth, the rocky peak that rises almost 1,900 feet above the pine forests and olive groves of the surrounding plain.

Chris continued narrating the story of Corinth, "In ancient and medieval times, an acropolis stood on the top of the pinnacle. The largest and oldest fortress in the entire Peloponnese, successive garrisons of Frankish, Byzantine, Venetian and Turkish soldiers once stood watch over the now-crumbling fortifications. Looking out over the sun-baked plains that stretched beneath them, each wave of invaders had known the triumph and tragedy experienced by occupation armies since men first began making war on each other."

Chris and Erika's route would carry them through three of the seven prefectures, or states, of the Peloponnese. Continuing south and west, they left the prefecture of Corinth and entered the fertile plains and golden valleys of the Argolid. Once the heart of Greece during the Mycenaean era around 1600 B.C., Argolis and its cities were heralded by some of Greece's most sublime voices—Homer, Sophocles, and Aeschylus.

"The region now is an agricultural center with fields of orange, lemon, and olive trees stretching from fortress-domed mountains to the crystalline coast on the Gulf of Argolis," concluded Chris.

The white Toyota motored through tiny villages and past roadside stands shaded by tall eucalyptus trees where farmers drank Greek coffee, played cards, and passed the time of day. Later in the summer, the stands would be heavy with grapes and apricots. The trees would be laden with grapefruit-sized oranges in the winter.

Erika continued to open up, offering more information about her job, her family, and her likes and dislikes. More than just polite conversation, Chris sensed that she was now speaking freely and comfortably. He felt she was genuinely enjoying herself.

As they approached the tiny village of Fihtes, Chris eased the Toyota off the highway in front of what appeared to Erika to be another *taverna*. Two old men, as gnarled and weathered as the olive trees in the countryside, sat at a table at the entrance. Despite the midday warmth, they wore wool sports jackets and v-neck sweaters, and both had woolen caps covering their heads. Their snow-white hair, eyebrows, and mustaches contrasted starkly with their burnt ochre complexions, the result of years of tending fields under a blazing Mediterranean sun.

"I thought we'd pick up a few things here for a picnic down the road near Mycenae," Chris said. "Want to get out for a few minutes?"

"Sure," said Erika, stretching. "Where are we, by the way?"

"Almost halfway. The rest of the drive is easier, though, because the big city traffic is behind us. Just these small villages down the coast road we'll be traveling."

The old men nodded and smiled as Chris and Erika walked past them into a small grocery store next to the *taverna*. Chris greeted them with the traditional *yia sas* and they smiled a response.

"It seems so strange to smile and speak to all these people we see," Erika said. "So easygoing and laid back. So different from our cities."

"No big city worries here," Chris smiled. "People actually make eye contact and talk to each other."

Chris picked up a loaf of homemade bread and a pound of black olives from the shelves. A plump young woman with rosy cheeks and salt-and-pepper hair sliced for him a chunk of feta off a large wheel of cheese and wrapped it in white paper. Erika went back out to the fruit display on the sidewalk in front of the store and picked out some peaches and bananas. She brought them into the store, where the attendant bagged them for her.

"This is all?" the lady asked.

Chris walked to a drink cooler and picked up a liter bottle of water and added it to their purchases. Erika offered her a handful of drachma notes, but Chris eased her hand aside.

"Come on now," she said. "I don't want to spend all this time here and not pay for anything. That's not fair."

"Sorry," Chris smiled. "Some things in Greece just aren't fair."

"Seriously, we're traveling together and I want to carry my share of the load."

"House rules. You're the guest here. My sisters would give me all kinds of grief if they saw me letting guests reach into their pockets. It's the Greek way."

The plump lady looked puzzled as to which money to accept. Chris ended the confusion by placing his money on the counter and speaking to her in Greek. She laughed, took his money, and gave him change.

"What did you tell her?" asked Erika as they left the store.

"Just that your money was no good."

"Yeah, I'll bet. Guess I'll be forced to learn this language just to keep up."

"That's a scary thought. Then I wouldn't have any way to keep a secret. By the way, I only picked up some water rather than sodas or beer because I want to stop down the road at my godfather's farm and get some of the fresh squeezed orange juice he makes from oranges from his own trees."

"I was going to ask you if there was anything besides water in the cooler back there. The juice sounds great."

They drove down the main road less than a mile and turned down a narrow lane shaded by huge eucalyptus trees that provided an almost perfect canopy. Orange and lemon groves stretched to the hills in the distance now shimmering in the heat. Men and women wearing broad-brimmed hats and long-sleeve shirts shielding themselves from the sun were returning to the scattered farm houses along the road after a morning of working in the groves. Following lunch, they would all stretch out in their homes for siesta until later in the afternoon, when the heat had somewhat subsided and they would venture out for a couple more hours in the fields before coffee time.

Chris turned into a gravel driveway leading to a small, white house with blue shutters and the traditional tile roof. Situated in a eucalyptus grove, the unshaded portion of the house literally assaulted the eyes with its dazzling whiteness, the result of the annual coat of whitewash all Greek houses receive just prior to Orthodox Easter. Flower boxes under each of the front windows held a rainbow of spring blossoms. An old blue Mercedes rested under a carport adjoining the house.

"This is absolutely beautiful," Erika said. "It's a picture right out of a travel brochure of Greece."

"Wait till you meet this man and his wife," said Chris as they got out of the car and walked to the house. "They are my godparents. They were very close to my mom and dad and came to the States to christen me when I was born. I always stop by and see them when I'm visiting Greece. They lived in the States for a couple of years, and he speaks pretty good English, but my godmother speaks almost none."

Chris knocked on the door as Erika investigated the flower boxes. She joined him at the door, and turned to look at the hills in the distance.

"What is all that up there?" she asked, pointing to two nearby hilltops, where a handful of tourists were poking around the rocks.

"That's part of the diggings at Mycenae, the ancient kingdom of Agamemnon," Chris replied. "There's an overlook there where I thought we'd have lunch."

Chris peered through the window next to the door. "I wonder where the old man could be?"

"Maybe they're not home," Erika said, walking to the side of the porch. She suddenly jumped back, startled at the figure that met her face to face from the side of the house.

"*Oriste*?" asked an old man under a huge straw hat.

"*Theo Spiro!*" Chris smiled, walking toward him with his arms outstretched. "*Ti mou kanis?*"

The old man looked past Erika at the figure approaching him as his puzzled expression suddenly became one of open-mouthed astonishment when he recognized Chris.

"*Christo!*" he cried. "*Christo mou!*" The old man's arms opened wide and embraced Chris, kissing him on both cheeks and spinning him around in a bear hug. Erika looked on with a smile of her own as the two hugged as only those with Mediterranean blood can greet each other.

"Uncle" Spiro was short, stocky, and even though he appeared to Erika to be in his 70s, he was powerfully built. He tossed his frazzled straw hat into a chair on the porch and a tussle of thick snow-white hair fell in a shower of curls around his face. His sunburned face held a two-day stubble of beard that promised to be as white as the hair on his head. A long-sleeved blue shirt buttoned at the collar and a pair of ancient baggy denim pants over his scruffy brown work boots completed his costume.

Erika smiled as she watched the two men hug each other. She noticed a hint of moisture from the old man's eyes crease its way across the weathered face.

"Uncle Spiro," Chris said, finally pulling himself out of the embrace, "I want you to meet someone."

He walked with the old man across the porch. "Uncle Spiro," said Chris with a hint of pride, "this is Erika. Erika, this is my Uncle Spiro."

"It is a pleasure to meet you, Uncle Spiro," Erika said, flashing her trademark smile and extending her hand. The old man opened his arms, however, and drew her to him in his own customary bear hug. Chris laughed when Erika's eyes grew wide as the old man embraced her like he was welcoming a member of his own family. Stepping back and holding her at arm's length, he virtually beamed as he looked at Erika.

"*Christo!*" he exclaimed without taking his eyes off her. "She is so beautiful!" Then he turned to Chris and began hugging him again, dancing around and laughing and rattling to him in Greek.

Chris's face began turning shades of red as he shook his head, responding to the old man's torrent of questions. They walked back to Erika, and from the sheepish look on Chris's face, she understood what the conversation was about.

"I don't speak any Greek," Erika said, "but I have a feeling I know what all the explanation centered around."

"Yeah, well," Chris stammered, "Uncle Spiro thought you and I were sort of married, and he was kind of excited about the news. I told him that we're just friends and we actually just met in Athens."

"Is no matter," the old man blurted out. "We so glad to meet you and to see Christo again. Three years now I don't see him. He too busy traveling around the world to come back to Greece."

"But you know the place I love the best, Uncle Spiro," Chris said. "Anyway, where is Aunt Alexandra?"

"She comes now," the old man said. "She's here in five minutes. I was in back washing up and heard you knocking on door. Wait till your *thea* sees you!"

He turned to Erika. "We love this boy very much," he said. "Me and my wife we never have children. Christo was like our son. I baptize him—I am his godfather. Me and his father like brothers."

Turning back to Chris the old man's eyes again became moist. "Older you get, more you look like Sam," he said. "You come for the wedding, yes?"

"You know I couldn't miss that," Chris said. "I met Erika in Athens and talked her into coming with me to Stavroula for a few days to see the wedding and a little bit of the country."

"This is my first time in Greece," Erika said. "I've always wanted to come here, and it looks like I have a tour guide now to show me the sights. You have a beautiful farm."

"*Koukla mou*," the old man said, taking her by the arm and walking her to the side of the porch, "this country grows two things easy—olives and rocks. Everything else takes hard work. We work plenty hard and now we have orange trees all the way to the hills there," he said, pointing to the hilltop ruins Chris had pointed out earlier. "Also lemons, olives, grapes, and the goats."

He called in Greek for his wife who now came into view

walking out of the orchard to a shed behind the house.

"*Ella, Alexandra*," he yelled. "Come see who is here."

They walked off the porch to the side of the house, the old man still with his arm protectively wrapped around Erika's shoulder. Chris followed behind them.

"Me, I speak good English," Uncle Spiro explained. "My wife, though, she not speak so good."

"I wish I could speak to her in Greek," Erika said.

"No worry, *Koukla*," he continued, "where Christo found you?"

"We met at Cape Sounion," Erika answered, amused at his choice of words.

"That I should know. That boy he always love Sounion. Even when little was his favorite place to visit in all of Greece. He told you about what he writes there after his mama died?"

"Well, no," Erika said, looking at Chris, "he didn't. Maybe he will show me later."

"Come on, Uncle Spiro," Chris said, "Erika and I just met."

"*Bravo*," the old man said. "Plenty of time for talk later."

Walking to the rear of the house they met the old man's wife returning from working in the orange groves. She, like her husband, was short, plump, and moved well for a woman of her years. Her cheeks, tinged by the sun despite her broad hat and scarf, glistened with a rosy glow offsetting two coal black eyes. She wore a faded gray dress that came just below her knees, and her legs were covered with the heavy black stockings favored by the older women in Greece's villages.

What most impressed Erika about the woman was her skin. Her face appeared to be as smooth as that of a woman half her age. Even when she smiled and her eyes became tiny squinting slits, there were no crow's feet around the corners. Nor was there a wrinkled brow or a sagging neck. Just a firm, taut, olive complexion that belied her years of working alongside her husband in the fields.

Recognizing Chris, she stopped in her tracks and threw open her arms. He walked straight up to her and drew her close to him, kissing her on each cheek.

"*Ti kanis, Thea*?" Chris asked, still holding the old lady.

She began a rapid fire litany in Greek until Chris, smiling and once again blushing, walked her over to Erika.

Erika laughed, assuming that he was again explaining their relationship and the fact that he was not bringing a new bride to meet the family.

"Erika," he said, "this is my Aunt Alexandra."

"It is a pleasure to meet you," Erika said, extending her hand and realizing at the last second that the gesture was futile. The old lady hugged her and stepped back to get a full picture.

"Hallo," she said demurely. "Welcome."

She looked Erika over carefully and began talking to Chris. The flush returned to his cheeks.

"She says it's a pleasure having you here," Chris said, "and she's also giving me hell for not phoning to tell her we were coming so she could have dressed to meet us. She also wishes she could speak English so she could talk to you. Plus a couple of other things."

"I can imagine," Erika said. "Please tell her I am pleased to meet her and Uncle Spiro just as they are. Oh, and tell her I am in love with her flowers and her farm."

Chris translated all this, and the old lady smiled and nodded, instructing him to relate additional information.

"Come, Christo," her husband interrupted. "We all go in the house and relax. Alexandra will fix us lunch."

"No, no, Uncle Spiro," Chris said. "We really don't have time right now. Maria and Sophia are expecting us in the village this afternoon. We wanted to stop by and say hello and pick up some of your famous orange juice. We plan on staying a few days in Stavroula, and I promise we'll be back to visit later."

"Okay, but only if you promise me," he said. Turning to Erika, he winked. "You make sure he keeps promise, eh *Koukla*?"

"I'll make sure, Uncle Spiro," Erika smiled.

"At least you stay for cold drink before you go, Christo," the old man said. "We go inside or you like better to sit out here on the patio?"

"It's so lovely here, why don't we sit on your patio?" Erika suggested.

"*Endaxi*," the old man said, motioning them to several chairs on a stone patio covered by a huge grape arbor. The leafy canopy along with two tall eucalyptus trees provided complete shade, and a slight breeze made the temperature delightful. Uncle Spiro began issuing instructions in Greek to his wife, who took Erika by the hand and headed for the back door of the house. Erika looked at Chris questioningly.

"She wants you to go with her inside and see the house," Chris said. "She'll also show you where the restroom is if you'd like to freshen up."

Chris and the old man settled in chairs on the patio. They talked for a few minutes, catching up on everyone. Then the old man leaned forward and placed his hand on Chris's knee and looked deep into his eyes.

"I see the way you look at this girl, Christo," he said. "Maybe you only just now meet her but maybe, too, something is happening, yes?"

"Come on, *Theo*," Chris began, "don't go reading anything here. I just invited her to come down here for a few days for the wedding and to see a little of the Peloponnesos. That's all. But she really is something, isn't she?"

"Like movie star she is! Maybe you say 'that's all' but don't try to fool an old man. Maybe we see what you don't say. Anyway, makes me feel so good you are here." He patted the knee again and smiled his most grandfatherly smile.

"Me too," Chris said. "You know how much I love you and *Thea* Alexandra."

The ladies came out of the house and Uncle Spiro immediately stood up and pulled a chair for Erika while Chris took the two large plastic bags that the old lady had for him.

"What's all this, *Thea*?" Chris asked. "We just want some juice to carry with us."

She began an animated explanation of the items she had collected and placed in the bags for him. Chris began a series of protests, entreating her to take some of them back, but the old lady was adamant. Finally Chris kissed her on the cheek, and they both sat down.

Uncle Spiro had moved his chair next to Erika, and was using an ancient walking stick to point out features of his orange groves and the hills in the distance. An admiral pointing out the positioning of ships in his fleet could not have been more proud. Aunt Alexandra had gone back into the house and returned with a tray that had a large pitcher of juice and four glasses with ice in them.

"Can I help with anything?" Erika asked.

"No, no," the old man said. "You sit. We have a glass of my juice."

His wife filled the four glasses and distributed them, giving the first glass to Erika.

The old man looked at Erika and raised his glass for a toast.

"In Greece, we say *e seyea*," he said. "Means peace and to your health."

They all raised their glasses and repeated the toast.

"Let me toast you and thank you for your hospitality," Erika said, raising her glass again.

They all clinked glasses again and took long drinks of the cold juice.

"Uncle Spiro, this is still the best orange juice in Greece," Chris said, winking at Erika.

"Forget Greece," the old man interjected. "Best in the world. Is good, eh, *Koukla*?" he asked Erika.

"It is wonderful," she said. The old man beamed.

They drained their glasses and talked for a few more minutes.

"Well," Chris said, finally rising from his chair, "we'd better be leaving."

They all rose and the old lady handed Erika one of the plastic bags. The other she gave to Chris. He put his arm around his godmother as they walked back to the Toyota. Uncle Spiro still had a protective arm around Erika, and she laughed as he continued relating childhood stories about Chris's visits to the farm.

Chris opened the Toyota and placed the bags on the back seat. Uncle Spiro whistled loudly at the amount of luggage already piled up there.

"You should see the trunk," Chris said. "This is only half of it."

"Just get in and quit making fun," Erika chided, giving Chris a light jab in the back. It was the second time she had touched him, and, again, it was electric.

Hugs and kisses on each cheek were followed by profuse thanks for the picnic items and promises to come back to visit. Chris and Erika finally got into the car and waved goodbye to the old couple standing in the front yard. Chris backed down the driveway and turned onto the road in the direction of the hilltop ruins.

"They really are wonderful people," Chris said, "and want to do everything in the world for us, but I hope they didn't come on too strong with the hugs and kisses. Sometimes strangers are a little put off by too much of that. It's just the way things are done here. Hope you weren't too uncomfortable."

"Hardly," Erika said. "Chris, I don't know if I've ever been made to feel more welcome in such a short period of time. They don't know me from Adam's house cat and yet, they couldn't do enough. They just make you feel so special."

"You are. You are a guest."

"If all the receptions are going to be like that one, I'm going to be spoiled rotten."

"I just don't want you to feel overwhelmed with family and crowds and visits. After all, this is supposed to be your vacation."

"I'll let you know if I feel closed in," she said. "I really enjoy people, and I have a feeling these will be some of the most interesting I have ever met."

"Get used to it then. There's a whole village full of stories."

Chapter Six

Chris had planned to stop for lunch at a place he remembered from visits he had made to the area with his father. There was a shady grove of trees which offered a grand view of the valley and the brooding ruins of Mycenae, the royal city of Agamemnon described in the poems of Homer. In the 1870s, the German archaeologist Heinrich Schliemann, intent on proving that Homer's epic works were more than just fiction, began excavating what he believed was the site of the ancient city. His efforts were rewarded when he triumphantly brought to light the long buried center of what had been Greece's most brilliant and powerful center of royalty until it was destroyed by fire in 1100 B.C. The palace complex, the royal tombs, and the sanctuaries, once laden with treasure pillaged from the extended wars of its rulers, were unearthed by Schliemann and stand now in mute testimony to their days of glory on the rocky hillsides overlooking the Argolid plain.

The ruins were located about three miles off the main highway along which Chris and Erika were traveling. Since Uncle Spiro's farm was roughly halfway between the junction and the entrance to the excavations, Chris had only about a mile and a half further to the picnic spot. Easing the Toyota off the road, he parked in a eucalyptus grove that had to have been designed by the Creator for moments such as this. A grassy area in the shade provided a good spot to stretch out and relax over a picnic lunch. Visitors would enjoy a view of the ruins and the hills to the north and a sweeping vista of the plain and gentler valleys to the south. The area was an incongruous mix of antiquity on the one hand and the fruits of modern irrigation on the other.

"You may be a writer, but you definitely have a photographer's eye for landscapes," Erika said. "I've got to get some pictures of this even with the midday light."

"Go ahead and shoot while I set up the lunch," Chris said.

"You won't believe how much stuff my aunt loaded us down with."

While Erika rummaged through her camera bag, loading film and changing lenses, Chris carried the grocery bags to a spot under one of the trees. Without a blanket or towel to serve as a tablecloth, he spread newspapers on the grass and anchored the corners with stones. He removed the bread, olives, cheese, and fruit from the bags and placed them on the paper. Aunt Alexandra's donations included a loaf of homemade bread, orange marmalade and juice, a jar of honey, paper plates, and an olive oil bottle filled with wine made from Uncle Spiro's own grapes. Chris smiled, thinking of the pride the old man took in each of his signature products—grapes, wine, orange juice, and marmalade from his own fruit trees.

After he had opened and spread the picnic items on the paper, he sat back against a tree and watched Erika. She had become totally absorbed in her photography, and was busy with light measurements, angles, and snapping her pictures. Completing the first roll of film, she picked up her second camera and continued shooting.

Chris noted her intensity. It was as if she had removed herself from her surroundings and was moving quickly and efficiently between shots, capturing different foregrounds, backgrounds, wide angles, and close-ups. Mesmerized again by her grace and beauty, he also noted her degree of professionalism and attention to detail as she numbered the shots in a notebook. She turned and smiled as she became aware he was studying her.

"What?" she asked, not expecting an answer.

"Just looking," he said.

"I will need for you to identify these shots for me so I can record them in my album, otherwise I won't know what I have here."

"No problem. I'll write it out for you, maybe even in English."

Erika smiled and returned to her photography.

Leaning back against the tree, he continued studying her. He had been with his share of attractive women in the past. Everyone had considered his ex-wife exceptionally beautiful as well as intelligent. But there was something about Erika that transcended all that. She was completely disarming. Not only to him, but, as he had noticed during the past two days, even in the eyes of others. The customers at the *taverna* in Sounion, the people in the lobby of the Hilton, the clerk in the grocery store, and, most recently, with Uncle Spiro and Aunt Alexandra. He decided Erika went far beyond attractive—she was positively stunning. And the most intriguing part of her mystique was that she was unaffected by it. There was something about women with exceptional good looks, and men too, for that matter, who knew they were striking. Many times it led to an attitude or a certain degree of narcissism. Those who seemed unconcerned or unaffected by their beauty became, to Chris, even more beautiful. Erika definitely fell into that category. Here was the consummate professional, he thought. Totally immersed in her work, obviously aware but not distracted by the effect she had on people. He seriously desired to know her better.

He again began to hunt for clues as to what she was trying to forget. The easiest approach would be simply to ask her what it was that triggered her mood swings, but he felt he didn't know her well enough for that. He would have to take it slowly and see if she opened up about her past. Maybe in the next few days, he thought, she might feel comfortable enough to talk about it. Meanwhile, just enjoy the moment.

When Erika completed her photography, she joined Chris under the trees. She dropped her camera bag and sat cross-legged across from him, whistling at the picnic spread before her.

"Wow!" she said. "They certainly don't want us to go hungry."

"Let's make a dent in it," Chris said, handing her one of the paper plates. He sliced some bread and cheese for her and piled her plate with marmalade, olives, and fruit. Then he passed her a cup.

"Juice or wine?" he asked.

"Better make it juice," she said. "A little early in the day for me."

"Juice it is," he said, filling her cup with the bright orange liquid. When he finished he raised his cup in a toast.

"What was the Greek word again?" she asked.

"*E seyea*," Chris answered.

"*E seyea*, then," Erika echoed. Taking a long drink, her eyes opened wide. "It's truly delicious."

They both began a spirited assault on the picnic items. Chris, who had always had a lively appetite, noticed that Erika took more than a passing interest in the cheese and olives, and stayed neck and neck with him in carving chunks of the bread spread with marmalade. Conversation centered around Erika's questions on the history of the area. She listened attentively to Chris's accounts of Schliemann's detailed studies of Homer's works to locate the exact spot where Agamemnon's city lay buried for centuries.

"This area is as interesting as it is beautiful," she said finally. "So peaceful and quiet after the hustle of Athens."

"That's exactly why Uncle Spiro loves it so much," Chris said. "He keeps a place in Athens, but you can't drag him away from here for long. How about some more juice or another piece of fruit?"

"Not a chance. I'm stuffed, and if we stay here much longer I'll be falling asleep. I think you Greeks may be on to something with this afternoon siesta business."

"See there," Chris said, "you're catching onto this lifestyle already."

Erika smiled and stretched her arms to the sky. "That's apparently pretty easy to do," she said. Leaning back against the tree, she appeared as much at ease as if they had known each other for years. Chris wanted to take a picture of her stretched out in the grass, but he decided not to ask. Keep it slow, he thought.

He found it difficult to maintain his concentration on their conversation. Lying on her side, facing him with her head propped on her arm, she was enchanting. The curve of her hips, her clinging T-shirt, and the blonde hair cascading over her shoulders were causing his head to swim. Chris felt like a starry-eyed high school kid. Wonder if I'm coming across like that, he thought.

He felt that their eye contact was becoming longer. He knew that his gaze was intense, and struggled to avoid any penetrating stares, but he found it difficult. Was it just his imagination or were her looks more inquiring? Or was it just wishful thinking?

Chris stood and stretched.

"Shall we pack up and get back on the road?" he asked.

"Let's do it," she said sitting up. Looking up at him, she smiled broadly. "Well, you've done great so far, Greek boy," she said playfully. "It's been a great morning."

"Glad you enjoyed it." He held out his hand and pulled her to her feet. Their eyes met again, and Chris felt like his face was on fire. He turned away as Erika smiled, aware of the effect she was having on him and amused at his surprising shyness.

They collected the remainder of their lunch and returned it to the plastic bags. Chris carried them back to the car and placed them in the rear seat while Erika gathered up the newspapers.

The afternoon drive carried them due south through a series of small villages surrounded by miles of orange, lemon, and apricot orchards and the ubiquitous olive trees. They skirted the ancient city of Argos that had reached its zenith six centuries before Christ, and is now a bustling farming community that serves as the agricultural and commercial center of the prefecture. Each of the surrounding peaks was crowned with the crumbling remains of Frankish and Venetian fortifications. Further south, the road became a series of serpentine twists and switchback turns hugging the coast of the Gulf of Argolis. The views from the cliffs overlooking the tiny bays and inlets were each more spectacular than the last. Erika asked Chris to stop several times for photographs, and he happily obliged. The usual hour and a half drive down the coast took them well over two hours, but they both had become totally oblivious to time. Erika was completely captivated by the scenery, and Chris delighted in watching her enthusiasm.

"This is some of the most beautiful scenery I have ever seen," Erika remarked. "And it seems like we are the only tourists here. I haven't seen a single tour bus since we left Corinth."

"It's not on the tourist trail, at least not for many Americans. The area is popular with Europeans looking for small beachside hotels and bed and breakfast places, but that's about it."

"This really is wonderful," she said, looking at Chris. "I would never have seen this if I had not decided to join you. I really appreciate it."

Chris felt his face ignite again. "Believe me, it's my pleasure," he said. "You've been great company."

"You make it sound like it's over."

"This part almost is. We are coming into Leonidion in a couple of minutes. From there we take the road up the mountain to Stavroula. We're almost home."

Erika noted with interest his choice of words.

Chapter Seven

After rounding what appeared to Erika to be the 100th hairpin turn on the coastal road, the town of Leonidion finally came into view. It was situated on both banks of an almost dry riverbed strewn with rocks and huge boulders. During the winter months, the river was a lively, tumbling waterway fed by the seasonal rains and snow melt from the mountains that rose almost perpendicularly from the north and south ends of the valley in which the town had grown up. The river was just a trickle now in the dry days of May, and would almost completely disappear later in July, not to be seen again until the rains came in November.

Hemmed in by the massive mountain ranges on two sides, the town had developed to the west through a valley that became successively narrower as it wound its way into the mountains. At the eastern edge was the ocean, rimmed by a string of rocky beaches where the river emptied into the Gulf of Argolis.

Crossing the first of a number of bridges that spanned the riverbed, they entered the narrow streets of Leonidion. The town was actually larger than Erika had expected. There was, naturally, a central square with *tavernas*, restaurants, a video club, grocery stores, and bakeries. In addition, they passed a bank, a central telephone office, a small medical facility, and two Greek versions of general merchandise stores. Chris pointed out two of the five Greek Orthodox churches in town. He also drove by the elementary and secondary schools which had recently let out for the day, and from which many of the students, in their blue pants and white shirts, were just now leaving. The younger of Chris's two sisters had attended this elementary school after the smaller one in the village had closed.

The houses in town ranged in size from small, whitewashed concrete block dwellings to large, two-story homes behind walls draped with flowers. Regardless of size, each had a well-tended garden with fruit trees, vegetables, and a grape arbor either along the side or at the rear of the residence. Small chairs and tables in the shade attested to the hours residents spent watching the world go by. As in all the villages they had passed, there did not appear to be any slums or depressed areas. Everything was small, but tidy and well kept.

The only objects of size were the mountains. They rose like lofty citadels almost 1,500 feet above the sea-level town. The afternoon sun burned the sandstone rock faces a burnt orange against the blue sky. The flat-topped peaks were criss-crossed by countless footpaths where shepherds for centuries had followed their herds of goats and sheep through the high country that was almost devoid of trees. The only vegetation in the dry, rocky cliffs were scrub bushes that somehow provided enough grazing for the hardy animals.

"This is exactly what I had imagined the small towns of Greece would be," Erika said. "It's like traveling across a postcard. I can't imagine what living here would be like."

"Definitely different from what we're used to. It's another world."

"That's it exactly. Back home we've grown accustomed to living behind burglar-alarmed doors in our neat little individual, air-conditioned worlds in front of a television. Rather than learning to interact with their friends, our kids spend their evening hours battling dragons in videogames. Here, people must spend hours sitting in the coffee houses around that park in the evening talking and relaxing rather than glued to a television. These kids can learn about life and living and how to get along in the world."

"That's pretty much all there is to do in these small towns. But I'm not sure these people are missing anything. I guess it's all about what you're used to. It's been like this for a long time. Times change and the world keeps turning, but I have a feeling that if we were to pop in here a hundred years from right now, we'd see the same thing."

As they drove on through the town, Chris pointed out some of the houses of friends and family who spent the winters in Leonidion. Each June, they migrated to their small homes in the nearby mountain villages to escape the heat of the summers in the lowlands. Erika noticed a few signs in English advertising rooms for rent and bed and breakfast facilities. Nothing, however, that would pass for a hotel.

In a few minutes they were on the other side of town. The road had become a level blacktop shaded by huge eucalyptus trees. On both sides were groves of orange and lemon trees. The ocean was in the distance about five miles away. Just as it appeared that they were heading straight for the small beachside guesthouses and restaurants, Chris slowed the Toyota and signaled a right turn.

"Are we going into the orange groves?" Erika asked.

"It looks like it," Chris laughed, "but up ahead is what passes for the only road into the mountains. We'll turn there and it's about six miles straight up to the village. You can say goodbye to paved roads for a while. It's a narrow dirt track from here on up."

Chris turned off the blacktop at a weathered, dust-covered sign that pointed to the right. The name of the village was in Greek letters with a ten kilometer sign next to it. The drive then became an adventure.

The narrow roadway had been graded, but that appeared to be the extent of the improvements it was ever likely to receive. Little rain had fallen since the winter, and the area was dry and dusty. Chris steered around rocks that seemed to come in two sizes—large and larger. The gradual climb was up a hillside flanked by olive trees that seemed to groan in the agony of their gnarled, twisted existence. A small farmhouse on the left of the road appeared to be the only permanent habitation in the area, but there were a number of shelters made of stone with limbs and branches serving as a roof.

"People don't live in those huts, do they?" Erika asked. "The area looks too affluent for people to be living in something like that."

"Those are shelters for the shepherds," Chris answered. "While their flocks graze, the shepherds will go inside them during the heat of the day for a nap. They'll also use them if a storm comes up."

Erika noticed the intricate construction of the shelters. While no mortar had been used to hold the rocks together, they had been arranged in such a manner as to give the appearance of construction by a professional stonemason. The walls were straight line symmetrical, and the stones were placed so perfectly together that they almost created a pattern. I guess you make do with the materials at hand, she thought. These people had learned centuries ago how to build without wood.

After about a mile the road twisted back on itself and began a steep climb. There was an excellent view of Leonidion with the ocean shimmering in the background. The afternoon light was now playing numerous tricks, with the orange cliffs highlighted by the lush green of the valley's irrigated fields. Erika began searching through her camera bag and loading film.

"I'm going to stop a little higher up," Chris said, "at an overlook which gives you a really nice view of the whole area. I'm glad there's not a lot of heat haze on the ocean. You'll have a nice clear backdrop of the whole vista."

"That is absolutely gorgeous," she said, looking back at the view as the road again zagged in the other direction. Turning back around, she could see the road ahead of them disappear in and around rocky promontories and outcroppings. The drop off on the passenger's side became a dizzying vertical plunge of almost 500 feet. Erika edged a little closer towards Chris.

"I guess guard rails here are out of the question," she commented.

Chris smiled. "First things first with the Greeks," he said. "It took them forever just to cut this road. Before that, it was just those little footpaths up the mountain. All the men in the mountain villages were expected to work a few weeks each year on the project until it was completed. The first automobile made the trip in 1958, and, believe me, it was quite an event. People tell me that everyone for miles around turned out for it. It really opened up the little mountain villages which had been so isolated for so long."

The Toyota seemed to wheeze slightly as Chris downshifted again to a lower gear. The next stretch of road was noticeably steeper as they climbed ever higher up the long grade. Another switchback brought them again to a point overlooking Leonidion. Wild valleys dropped precipitously off to one side while a series of mountain ranges faded to blue in the distance. And behind them was the ocean, ever present no matter how far the traveler feels he has penetrated the interior of Greece.

Chris stopped the car at a point just off the road with a sweeping view of the valley, the mountains, the town, and the ocean. As he switched off the engine and set the parking brake, Erika was already out of the car.

He watched as she walked to the edge of the cliff with her camera bag slung over her shoulder and the breeze blowing her hair. She stood with her hands on her hips drinking in the panorama. He had seen the same view from the same spot a thousand times, but never had it captured him as it did at that moment. I guess it's different with someone in the picture frame, he thought. He got out of the car, walked to the edge of the cliff and stood beside her.

"This takes the breath away," she said, looking out over the valley. "I don't know if I have ever seen anything so beautiful." She turned to face him and her face was beaming. "We've got a few minutes for some photos, don't we?" she asked. She seemed like a child wanting one more ride on the roller coaster.

"You bet," Chris said. "Time is the one thing we do have plenty of around here. Besides, we're on 'holiday'". He used the word with a distinct British accent, the way Europeans talk about their vacations.

He sat on a rock and watched her shoot the scene from different angles with different lenses. The breeze had picked up slightly and was blowing her hair in a way that reminded him of an action photo taken at a slow shutter speed to blur the subject. He was almost disappointed when she returned to the car to retrieve her hat and pull it low over her face to keep the hair out of her eyes. After shooting almost two rolls of film, she turned around and started framing him for a few shots.

"Now there's a shot," she said as she clicked away. "The Greek Adonis on his throne overlooking his kingdom. Any instructions for your subjects, m'lord?"

Chris laughed. "Yes, back to the chariot and let's get up to the castle. I'm getting excited now that we're almost there. I can't wait for you to see the place."

They walked back to the car, and she paused a second to look around before opening the door.

"It just feels like we are light years away from the rest of the world," she said. "This country appears so wild and rugged and empty. There's not even any sound except for the wind. It's as if we're the only people on an artist's landscape."

"Maybe not the only ones, but certainly among just a handful," Chris said. "The solitude here wraps you like a blanket."

"I'm liking it already," she exclaimed excitedly. She opened the door and bounced into the car, tossing her camera bag in the back seat. "Let's go, what are you waiting on?" she called.

Chris laughed, got in, and started the car. The Toyota hesitated slightly as they began the climb again, as if it knew that the steepest part of the ascent lay ahead. The next couple of miles were a series of tortuous switchbacks along a narrow track that had been blasted out of the solid rock face of the mountain. Weaving around some of the larger rocks that had become dislodged and rolled into the road brought them on several occasions a little closer to the edge than Erika would have liked. Looking over the side, the world dropped away into a rock chasm filled with the ubiquitous scrub brush that covered the hillsides. Chris pointed out the trail that had been the only access to the village prior to construction of the road in the 1950s.

The switchbacks came faster now as they neared the top of the grade. Suddenly, they were on top of the peak and on a dirt road that ran along the level plateau on which the village of Stavroula was situated. Rather than being on top of the mountain, however, Erika noticed that there were peaks around them that rose another couple of hundred feet higher. Still there was no sign of the village. She noticed the definite odor of livestock, however.

A half mile further along the summit road they encountered their first signs of life. A herd of goats was crossing in front of them to a watering area that had been constructed on a low rise just off the road. A young man who appeared to be in his early 20s was in the road moving them along, and he looked up to see the car approaching. He used his walking stick to prod the slow movers to catch up with the others already around the concrete cisterns fed by a series of metal chutes from a central watering station. An old man wearing a pair of incredibly faded gabardine pants, a tattered wool sport coat, and the traditional black wool sailor's hat stood with his walking stick next to the goats at the well.

Chris stopped the car and began talking in Greek to the young man. Immediately, he began laughing and gesturing with both hands, first towards the village and then to the old man. He called to the old man, whose face became animated and broke into a smile revealing a mouth containing no more than half the teeth it once had. Chris waved to him and spoke to them both in Greek for a moment and pointed to Erika. A bilingual introduction followed, and Erika smiled and waved at the herdsmen. Chris waved a final goodbye and continued on the road.

"What an incredible picture that would make," Erika said, looking back at the men still waving from their perch by the well. "I didn't really feel comfortable asking if I could photograph them. Do you think it would be okay later on? I would really love to capture some of these faces."

"Not a problem," Chris said. "They'd be flattered, especially if you were in some of the shots with them. I brought my video camera for the wedding and the parties. They really get a kick out of seeing themselves."

The summit road was surprisingly flat and ran straight for about a half mile before veering off to the right into a grove of cedar trees. Just before the turn, Chris pulled to the side of the road and switched off the engine.

"Just one more quick stop," he said. He got out of the car and walked to a blue metal shrine about the size of a large box on the side of the road. There was a cross on top, and behind a glass door were a few icons of saints, several weathered family photographs in ancient, rusting frames, a few candles, a Coca Cola bottle half filled with olive oil, several books of matches, and a glass containing a handful of Greek coins. Erika joined Chris at the shrine and watched as he opened the small glass door and made the sign of the cross in the fashion of Orthodox Christians. He took a match and lit one of the candles. He looked at the items in silence for a minute, then crossed himself again, and closed the tiny door.

"These little roadside shrines are all over Greece," he explained. "Sometimes a person erects one in honor of a saint or a family member. Sometimes it's to give thanks and other times just to remember a wife or husband or something. My parents built this one back in the 1950s in honor of my grandfather on my father's side. He died during the war fighting the Italian occupation troops in a village nearby. The icon is of Saint Michael, my grandfather's name and the patron saint of soldiers. People stop by these things from time to time and say a prayer, straighten the things up inside, refill the olive oil lamp, and leave some change."

"It's beautiful," Erika said. "Do you mind if I take a picture?"

"Of course not. Help yourself. Should look good with this late afternoon light."

Erika took a few pictures, and they walked back to the car. Chris was impressed that she first asked about taking pictures of the shrine and how she appeared quiet and almost reverent at the site.

"I never knew my grandfather," he said, "but I've heard lots of stories about him from my parents and many of the people in the village. His name is on the memorial the people of Stavroula erected to the men from the village who died in all the wars of this century."

"Are there more of these little shrines around here?"

"Yes, I had one built for my parents on a hilltop overlooking the village. We can hike up there one day while we're here if you like. It's a beautiful spot with a great view."

"Seems like there is no shortage of them around here. Everywhere you look is a postcard setting."

"Well, get ready for the main one. The village is just around that next bend. We're almost home."

She smiled and again noticed his choice of words.

Chapter Eight

The road divided as it entered the village, and Chris took the fork to the right. The town consisted of a cluster of white stone houses with the traditional red tile roofs nestled among pine and cedar trees that provided the only color in the rocky landscape. They passed a tall white marble monument in a shady grove on the left and an old building with a fenced playground on the right. A frayed soccer goal was the sole reminder of the days when the village children passed their after-school hours practicing the skills which they dreamed would one day put them on one of Greece's national teams.

"That's the old school," Chris said. "It's closed now as there are so few families still living here. Most of the younger families have moved down off the mountain looking for jobs in the cities. It's mostly the old folks who have remained."

The narrow serpentine road wound down a hill past a few houses with wire enclosures for chickens and goats. At the bottom of the hill they turned right and stopped the Toyota.

"Now we walk," Chris said. "The house is just around the corner, but the streets are too narrow for cars."

They left the Toyota in the shade of a huge fig tree, and walked up a narrow lane flanked by brilliantly whitewashed houses and equally brilliant stone fences on both sides of the path. Flaming bougainvillea of red, pink, purple, and white grew from the yards onto the second-story balconies of the houses, almost creating a canopy under which Chris and Erika strolled. Most houses had flower boxes in the windows adding to the delirium of color that welcomed them. Erika suddenly stopped in her tracks.

Chris turned around, puzzled. "What's the matter?" he asked.

"I don't believe this," she said. "Is this not the most beautiful sight you have ever seen? Look at the colors of those bougainvillea. I have never seen anything so lovely in my entire life! The air is positively intoxicating with the scent of all those flowers. And the houses are dazzling. It's magnificent!"

Red chrysanthemums in huge clay pots peeked at them from their niches next to the doors of the homes. Several sleepy cats lounged in the shade, barely noticing the newcomers who dared interrupt their naps.

Chris stopped for a second in front of a weathered door opening into a flower-filled courtyard. "Here we are," he said. "Ready for all this?"

"Ready as I'll ever be," she said.

They entered the courtyard and walked up a short flight of concrete steps onto a porch bursting with chrysanthemums, geraniums, sunflowers, and flanked by the most aromatic mint and basil Erika had ever encountered. She felt almost hypnotized by the scent and the beauty as Chris knocked on the door and gently pushed it open.

"Anybody home?" he called. "What kind of greeting is this with nobody around?"

Shouts of "Christo! Christo!" emanated from the kitchen and the rear of the home as two young girls raced into the living room and jumped into Chris's arms as he whirled them around amidst hugs and kisses. A slender woman wearing a white apron over her blue housedress and a white kerchief covering her head emerged from the kitchen and joined the girls in embracing Chris and showering him with kisses.

The girls virtually squealed with delight when they noticed Erika standing behind him, and they stepped back, smiling demurely at the stranger. Chris finally pulled himself away from the women and rattled on for a minute in Greek as he motioned to Erika and held out his hand urging her in from the foyer. She walked forward, smiling.

"Erika," Chris said, "this is my sister, Maria, and these are her daughters, Irene and Anna. Girls, this is my friend, Erika."

"Erika, is so nice to meet you," Maria said, wiping her hands with the towel and taking Erika's extended hand in hers. She removed the scarf from her head and a shock of dark hair with the first streaks of gray tumbled to her shoulders. "I could kill this brother of mine for not telling me he was bringing company so I don't look like this." She pretended to beat Chris with the towel much to the delight of the young girls.

"It's a pleasure to meet you, Maria," Erika said. "And please don't worry about me being company. I met Chris in Athens and he talked me into coming here to meet all of you and see a little bit of Greece with him. I've really been looking forward to it. I hope it's not an imposition."

"No, no, no!" Maria assured her. "We have plenty of room." She took her arm and led her into the house. "Here, the girls can show you where you can freshen up after your trip and we get your bags." The young girls led Erika down the hall to the bathroom and opened the door for her.

"Little brother," Maria began, "why you don't tell me?" She slid her arms playfully around his neck, pretending to be choking him.

"I really didn't have time," Chris laughed. "Everything happened so fast in Athens. We met at Sounion, and I wasn't even sure she was going to come with me. It just happened."

"Is anything 'happening'?" she asked, smiling. "She is very beautiful."

"That I don't know," he smiled. "I'll tell you all about it later."

"I don't think you need to tell me too much. I see your eyes how you look at her. I think maybe the, how you say, 'love bug', he bites my baby brother, no?"

"Maria, you know me better than I know myself," Chris said, walking to the door. "I'm going to get our bags out of the car."

The girls raced into the room taking their uncle's hands and walked with him onto the porch. They accompanied him to the car, teasing and laughing with Chris and bombarding him with questions about himself, Erika, and his life in general. Growing up in a small town in rural Greece, they came to relish Chris's visits. Each time he returned, he came laden with gifts and souvenirs from some exotic corner of the world along with travel stories that fascinated them for hours. Their globetrotting uncle who lived in the States had been a hero to them for as long as they could remember.

When Erika emerged from the bathroom, Maria showed her to a comfortable guest bedroom with a large bed, a chest of drawers, and a closet. A heavy comforter and a colorful afghan lay folded at the foot of the bed. The room's two windows had blue wooden shutters, and opened to a magnificent view of the village with the mountains falling away in the distance. A tiny white church was perched on the crest of the closest peak. Chris and the girls brought in the bags and placed Erika's things in her room. The girls smiled at each other as Chris stowed his gear in a smaller bedroom down the hall. Returning to the kitchen, he found Erika helping Maria lift a huge pan with a roast leg of lamb from the oven to the kitchen table.

"Already putting our guest to work?" he asked.

"She wants to help so she helps," Maria quipped. "Everyone comes tonight for dinner at eight o'clock. But we are almost ready."

"It looks like you're expecting the legions of Rome," Erika said. "I can't believe all this food."

"Maria, where is Ted?" Chris asked.

"At the *kafenion*. Why you don't get out of our way and go find him? Maybe Erika wants to go too and see the village?"

"No, no," Erika protested. "I'm fine right here learning about cooking all this food. You go ahead and you can show me the sights tomorrow."

"I'm gone," Chris said. He turned to Irene and Anna. "Ladies," he began, "I think there might just be a few things in my bags with your names on them. I'll have a look when I get back and see if I remembered to bring them or gave them to the gypsy children down in Leonidion."

They instantly began begging him in Greek to get their gifts now, but Chris smiled and waved them away.

"Later," he said. "I'll be back before you know I'm gone."

The girls joined Erika and Maria in the kitchen as Chris left the house. Closing the courtyard door behind him, Chris turned down the narrow lane leading to the *kafenion*, which was located in the center of the village. The village streets, most of which were narrow paths just barely wide enough for a single car, radiated from the coffee house. It served, along with the church, as the hub of activity for the tiny community.

Chris passed the familiar houses along the way. He remembered the families living in each one, and wondered if their owners had already arrived to spend the summer or had not yet left Athens in their annual exodus to escape the city's heat and tourist crowds. The melancholia that overtook him each time he returned to Stavroula began to creep up on him now. Remembering the local people brought back a flood of memories for him. Thoughts of his parents, weddings, baptisms, Easter celebrations, annual festivals, the old timers of the village—they all returned now to remind him of the wonderful days he had spent here. In his mind's eye, these treasured pictures were as clear to him now as they were when they unfolded. So many were now gone. So much had changed. He had his life in the States. He had gone off to college, off to war, tried his hand at marriage, and traveled around the world. But Stavroula was always the same. He could close his eyes and negotiate through every street in town. The little village was always the same. In a world of change and uncertainty, he could always count on it to remain. Maybe this is my security blanket, he thought. My link to the past.

He was snatched back to the present by a tall, slim, solitary figure coming around the corner from the coffee house. He recognized the man immediately as Ted, his brother-in-law.

"*Ti kanis, Thodori*?" Chris called to him in Greek.

Ted stopped for a second and, recognizing Chris, broke into a huge smile. He hurried forward and put his sack on the ground as the two men embraced and went through the traditional kiss-on-each-cheek greeting.

Ted had been working in his olive groves that morning, and still wore his faded denim pants with a sweat-stained long-sleeved white shirt. Unlike most of the men and women in the village who worked in the fields, Ted never wore a hat. He was in his early fifties and his face was bronzed and deeply creased, reflecting his years of working outside. Ted understood some English, but spoke almost none at all. Their conversations, therefore, were mostly in Greek. He asked Chris how he had been, how long he would be staying, what was new in his life, and all the usual catching up questions. Chris answered each of them, and he told him about Erika. Ted was still prodding Chris for information on his new friend as they walked up the stairs to the house.

The remainder of the afternoon was a mélange of unpacking bags, distributing the gifts that Chris had brought for everyone, and getting ready for the evening's dinner guests. By the time Chris had showered and joined the family on the front porch, it was almost 7:30. Maria had opened one of the large bottles of Amstel beer purchased at the coffee house and poured a glass for Ted and one for her brother. Chris felt that relaxing on the flower-filled patio of his sister's house in the village in the early evening with a cold beer was another item on his list of life's great pleasures. Right on up there with his Snickers bars. Catching up on the news of the family was the icing on the cake. It doesn't get much better than this, he thought.

He was wrong. Erika and the two young girls emerged from the house, and Chris's heart skipped a beat. The girls held her hands as the trio walked outside and looked around smiling. Ted was as starstruck as Chris. He stood up for the introductions.

Erika wore white linen pants and a yellow jacket over a high necked, black cotton blouse. Her blonde hair was pulled slightly back and held with a white ribbon. The gold chain with a small cross that she wore around her neck shone even brighter against the black blouse. Her blue eyes sparkled with their usual brilliance. Maria glanced at Chris, who appeared mesmerized.

"You clean up well, lady," Chris smiled after recovering his wits.

"Amazing what a shower can do," she smiled. Turning to Ted, she extended her hand. "Hello," she said, "I'm Erika."

"Ted, this is my friend Erika," Chris said. "Erika, my brother-in-law, Ted."

"A pleasure," Ted said in his broken English. "Welcome." Then he looked at Chris.

"Erika," Chris began, "Ted doesn't speak much English but wants you to know how happy he is that you're here. Anything you need, just let him or the girls know."

"Thanks so much for your hospitality," Erika smiled at Ted. "Everything is lovely."

They took seats around the table on the porch, and Maria appeared with a serving tray. She gave Erika a glass of white wine and poured one for herself. The girls each had a glass of Coke. They all raised their glasses and Ted, as the head of the household, proposed a toast.

"He said the equivalent of 'welcome, good health, and long life'," Chris translated. They clinked their glasses and sipped their drinks.

"*E seyea*", Erika said with a smile, attempting her first Greek word and offering her toast.

They all laughed their approval, repeated her Greek toast, and drank again.

Conversation centered around their trip from Athens, what Erika's career was like, Chris's latest travels, and how Ted's olive and orange trees were doing. The girls pored over the American fashion magazines Chris had brought them. Soon, the hors d'oeuvres tray of feta cheese and olives was almost empty. The hypnotic aroma of the roasted lamb and the other delicacies emanating from the kitchen was causing Chris's stomach to growl in anticipation.

"I'm starving," he finally said. "What time did you say the company's coming?"

"Relax, little brother," Maria said. "They come at eight o'clock. You know we don't eat dinner so early as you in America."

Just as she finished her statement, the gate to the courtyard opened and the guests arrived. About a dozen people filed into the yard, led by an old man and old lady who, Erika assumed, were the grandparents. They were the quintessential image of the Greek villagers. The old man had a thick head of silver hair and wore a heavy woolen sweater over a pair of gabardine slacks. His wife had one of the loveliest countenances that Erika felt she had ever seen. Rosy cheeks, a happy smile, and dark hair pulled back in a bun. Not a flick of gray on her head. The guest of honor and his fiancée followed along with their parents.

The traditional hugs, kisses, and introductions followed. Maria and the girls went into the kitchen for drinks and hors d'oeuvres while Chris, Ted, and the guests arranged additional chairs on the porch. Erika followed the girls into the kitchen, and, despite Maria's urging to return to the porch, stayed to help with the drinks and the trays. When they returned to serve the guests, Chris explained to her who the people were.

There was Andreas, the cousin about to be married, and Eleni, his fiancée. Both their parents were there, along with Andreas's grandfather and grandmother. In addition, Andreas's younger brother and Eleni's two younger sisters were there. All now lived in Athens, where the couple had met. Andreas was an architect and Eleni worked as a loan manager at a bank.

After what seemed to Chris like an eternity, it was time for dinner. The party moved down the steps to a corner of the courtyard that had been set up with several long tables set end to end and covered with white tablecloths. High backed wooden chairs were behind each of the eighteen plates and table settings set up for the dinner. While the men sat and poured wine, beer, and sodas that had been chilling in two huge metal washtubs filled with ice, the women went into the kitchen to begin shuttling the plates piled high with food.

Seated next to her, Chris explained to Erika each individual dish. There were two roast legs of lamb simmering in their own juices and seasoned with oregano and small cloves of garlic. Next came several huge platters of *pastichio*, the Greek version of lasagna, with layers of ground meat, macaroni, and cheese. The next plate coming was loaded with *moussaka*, the version of *pastichio* that added eggplant along with the ground meat. Bowl after bowl of the roasted Greek potatoes, marinated in spices, were accompanied by fresh greens from Ted's garden. Two giant serving bowls held the traditional Greek salad of tomatoes, cucumbers, and onions in a light olive oil dressing. Even with all the guests' plates piled high, there were still mounds of food in the serving platters.

After everyone was served, the grandfather offered a blessing in Greek. Then the bridegroom-to-be offered a toast that Chris translated for Erika. He drank to the good health of the host family and thanked them for the dinner party. Then he turned to his fiancée and thanked her for making him the happiest man in the world. They all clinked their glasses and the meal began.

Conversations buzzed all around them. Politics, travel, what's happening in Athens, what's happening in the States. Chris wanted to spend more time talking to Erika, but she was being bombarded with as many questions as he was receiving himself. She appeared to him to be holding her own.

Halfway through the meal he turned to her and smiled.

"Everything okay?" he asked.

"Just fine," she smiled. "The food is great and the company is wonderful."

"You sure?"

"You bet. Except for the older couple, just about everybody speaks a little English. I'm getting along just fine. This is really an experience."

"Looks like you've made some new friends."

"These people are incredible. I gave the girls a few magazines that ran some of my pictures. They've brought them to me to autograph. I feel like some kind of celebrity."

"You are. They are all convinced you're some kind of movie star. Far be it from me to shatter any illusions."

A renewed flurry of questions and conversations tugged at both of them for the remainder of the meal. When the feeding frenzy was finally over, the young girls went into the kitchen and returned with trays of Greek pastries for dessert. Maria put coffee on for the coffee drinkers, and Ted refilled the wine and beer glasses. Irene, Anna, and Eleni's two younger sisters cleared the dishes and disappeared into the kitchen. It was almost 10:30 by the time the last cup and glass were drained. Conversation continued for another half-hour before Andreas's grandfather, the patriarch of the family, pushed back his chair and stood up, signaling that it was time to go.

The hugs and kisses were repeated as all took part in the requisite routine for leaving the home of the host. By the time the last guest had left the courtyard and closed the gate, Anna and Irene had already cleared the remaining coffee cups and dessert plates. Chris and Ted put the tablecloths in a large plastic bag, and began breaking down the tables. Maria, Erika and the girls washed and dried the last of the plates and put them away. They joined Chris and Ted on the patio.

"Great job, ladies," Chris said. He went on to brag about how much work Anna and Irene had done in helping their mother, and he tussled with them in his chair.

"It really was a wonderful dinner and party," Erika said. "Maria, you are a wizard in the kitchen. I would love for you to write some of those recipes down for me."

"I will be happy to," Maria said, "but I think now we are ready for sleep. We had big day today and tomorrow night is big party after the wedding." She turned to the girls. "Girls, say goodnight to everybody and off you go."

Irene and Anna each gave their father a goodnight hug and kiss. Then they hugged their Uncle Chris, and he picked them up and held them over his head amidst squeals of delight.

"Goodnight, *koukles*," he said. His reference to them as "dolls" had always won their hearts. They each hugged Erika before scampering into the house.

"It's been a long day for us too," Chris said. "Erika, I know you must be tired."

"I am," she said, "but after that huge meal I think I might like a walk around the block. You up for it?"

"Sure," Chris said. "It's almost a full moon too. C'mon, let's walk up to the church and I'll give you the ten-minute tour of the village."

"You go for your walk, we go to bed," Maria said, rising and pulling Ted up from his chair also. "Erika, you know where is everything you need, yes?"

"I sure do, Maria. Thanks again for a lovely evening. See you in the morning."

Chris hugged his sister and put his arm around Ted's shoulder and walked them to the door. He bade them "*kali nihta*", the Greek goodnight. "Do you want your jacket?" he asked Erika. "Still pretty chilly at night here even this late in May."

"Not chilly, cold!" Erika corrected him. "I'm getting my jacket for sure."

Chris slipped his jacket on, and walked down the steps into the courtyard. He looked up at the night sky and watched the show in the heavens. There were no neon signs or miles of highway lights to drown out the stars up here, he thought. The moon was one night away from being full, and its position in the sky served to bathe the neighboring houses in a shadowy brilliance.

"You could almost read out here, it's so bright," Erika said, walking up behind him. "What an incredible night." She took his hand and they walked toward the gate. Again, Chris was electrified.

She opened the doorway, and they walked down the narrow lane. The moonlight was casting eerie shadows from the silent houses. Even the animals seemed to be sleeping. Not a sound came from the pens where the goats and chickens were housed. A small orange bulb shining over one of the porches appeared to be the only artificial light in the neighborhood. A dog barking in the distance on the other side of town was the only sound.

"I feel like we're the only people here," Erika whispered softly as if to preserve the silence.

"We're about the only ones awake," Chris replied. "There's probably a few still sitting in the coffee house. Just about everybody has turned in."

They turned the corner and walked a block up the hill to the church. It was built on what appeared to be the high point of the village. A small structure, it nevertheless had a high round dome with a cross on top that looked to be almost spotlighted by the moonglow. Chris pointed out the rows of stained glass widows that looked almost black with no backlight to highlight their rainbow of colors.

Chris picked up a stick from the roadside and played with it as they walked down the hill leading to the old school where they had first entered the village that afternoon. He stopped at the low fence surrounding the white marble monument in the middle of the small park across from the school.

"That's the memorial to all the men from the village who have died in the various wars of this century," he explained. "It has about forty names on it dating back from the time of the Balkan Wars through World War II. My grandfather's name is on it."

He opened the gate and walked through. "It's kind of like our Vietnam Veterans Memorial only it's dedicated to a whole series of wars rather than just one conflict." He stopped when he noticed Erika was not following him. Looking back, he saw she had stopped at the gate and had turned around and was facing the school. He walked over to her.

"Are you okay? What's the matter?" he asked.

Erika kept her eyes fixed on the school. "I'm all right," she answered finally.

"Erika, what's the matter? You seem to be all of a sudden in some other place. It was the same back in Athens. Is it something I said or did?"

She turned to face him, the moonlight bathing her high cheekbones, full lips, and incredible eyes. "Chris, I have a thing about places like this," she said. "It's a long story that maybe later I'll tell you, but not now. Not here. This place is too wonderful and this day has been too perfect. Okay?"

Chris looked deep into her eyes and thought he detected a hint of moisture there. "Of course," he said. "I don't want you to talk or think about anything that upsets you. If I have…"

"You haven't," she interrupted. "You've been great. I am really glad I made the trip with you to this place. It's everything I thought it would be. And your family is wonderful. It's not you, it's me. I'll tell you about it later."

The somber mood seemed to leave her as quickly as it came.

"Right now," she smiled, "it's getting cold and I'm getting sleepy."

"Then let's head for home," Chris said, taking her hand and turning to leave.

She held his hand, but didn't move. When he turned back around she pulled him to her and put her arms around him. She drew his face to her and kissed him eagerly on the lips. Confused and shocked at first, Chris melted at her touch and returned the kiss with a passion. They remained locked in an embrace for a long moment before Erika pulled slowly away and smiled at him. Chris's face was again on fire.

"Thanks for a great day, Greek boy," she whispered. "Do all you Greeks kiss like that?"

Chris hesitated for a moment before answering her. "Only when we're in over our heads," he answered. "I can't tell you how glad I am you're here."

"It's been a great start," Erika smiled. She pulled away from him slowly and took his hand, leading him down the road to his sister's house. They talked about the stars during the few minutes it took to get back to the house, but Chris's mind was nowhere near the conversation.

Entering the courtyard, he closed the gate and they walked together up the stairs. He stopped at the doorway and turned to face Erika. He kissed her lightly on the lips and on her forehead.

"Goodnight," he whispered. "See you in the morning."

"Sleep tight," she said. "Thanks for a great day."

They kissed again—another long, passionate kiss, and Chris was almost delirious holding her against him. Then they pulled apart. She opened the door, waved at him, and smiled her most devastating smile. He watched her walk down the darkened hall and close the door to her room behind her. Chris walked to his room and turned on the light. Taking off his jacket, sweater, and jeans, he tossed them on the chair and hopped onto his bed. He clasped his hands behind his neck and stared at the ceiling, his heart still pounding. He still tasted her, smelled her, felt her. Never in my life, he thought. Never has anything or anybody affected me like this. And she was the one who initiated the kiss! But what was it again that drew her into her sudden mood swings? What was it about the memorial or the mention of wars that gripped her? He felt like he was getting close to an answer. She even said she'd explain later. For now, that kiss in the moonlight and their embrace would be enough to fill his dreams as he drifted off to sleep.

Chapter Nine

Chris opened his eyes and looked at the clock on the stand beside his bed. Almost 8:30. He stretched and yawned, but made no attempt to get up. Staring at the ceiling, he recounted the events of the previous night, especially their walk through the village. And that long, passionate kiss and embrace in the moonlight that left him breathless. It actually happened, he thought. That was no dream.

He pulled a pair of denim shorts from his bag and pulled them on. Without a shirt or shoes, he walked down the hall and heard voices in the kitchen. Peeking through the doorway, he smiled a big hello to Maria and Erika sipping coffee at the table.

"Up already?" he asked.

"What do you mean, already?" Erika countered. "Seems like you're the only late sleeper here. We've already had our coffee."

"Good morning, little brother," Maria said, walking over to her brother and kissing him on the cheek. "You slept well?"

"After I finally got to sleep," he said, looking at Erika who smiled and blushed.

"Really?" Maria said. "That's not like you. Most of the time you are sleeping when your head hits your pillow." She smiled slightly, trying to appear confused as to what could possibly have kept him awake. "The girls are still asleep, but Ted left early this morning for Leonidion. He needed to do some work on his olive trees and to run for me some errands. Why you don't go and take shower before you come in here? You look like wild man."

"I'm on my way," Chris laughed. "What are the plans for today?"

"Only plan is for wedding tonight and the reception after," Maria replied. She looked at Erika. "Will be dinner, bouzoukia, dancing, everything."

"I've heard so much about the Greek weddings," Erika said. "I'm really excited about getting to actually go to one."

"What time tonight?" Chris asked.

"For us is 6:30 at church," Maria answered, "because Irene and Anna will be in the wedding. Wedding is at seven o'clock."

"That's great, Chris interjected. "It gives us all day to hike and explore the area and show Erika some of the world's greatest views."

"Maria, are you sure there's nothing I can help you do?" Erika asked.

"Nothing, nothing," she waved a response. "Last night was only thing for me. We wanted Andreas and Eleni and the family to come for dinner because we always close friends with them. Now, except for Irene and Anna in the wedding, we will be like all other people there. Will be very good time. You and my little brother go walking in the mountains. And you don't let him tell you he's lost," she smiled. "He knows very well the mountains around this place."

"Why, big sister," Chris exclaimed, "I can't believe you would think I would try an old-fashioned trick like that. Especially now that I'm on my best behavior."

"Just go get cleaned up," Erika laughed. "I have a pretty good sense of direction, and I certainly don't want to miss the festivities tonight. I really enjoyed last night."

"I'll just be a minute," Chris said as he headed down the hall to the bathroom.

Erika left the kitchen and went to her room, where she changed into a pair of tan khaki shorts and a white T-shirt. She laced up her hiking boots and brushed her hair, deciding that a ponytail would best serve her during the day. She put a tube of sunscreen along with her camera and several rolls of film into her backpack. Looking in the mirror, she put her baseball cap on and pulled the ponytail through the opening in the back. Satisfied that everything was in place, she slung her pack over one shoulder and walked back to the kitchen.

Chris was drinking his coffee and munching on some bread that Maria had toasted for him in the oven.

"You've gotta try this," he said, offering her a piece of the warm bread with a pat of butter melting over the top. "Put a little of the fig preserves on it. Maria makes this herself from the figs from her trees."

"Yes, but last year the figs don't do so good," Maria said as she rinsed some glasses in the sink. "This year maybe they do better."

"Wow," Erika exclaimed, "this is delicious! And the bread is fabulous. Is it homemade too?"

"She bakes it herself in the oven in the yard," Chris said proudly. "Best homemade bread in Stavroula."

"I would love to watch you if you're going to bake some in the next few days," Erika said. "I'd really like to see how it's done in the outdoor oven."

"Sure," Maria said. "We fix some maybe the day after the wedding."

"Maria, when is Sophia getting here?" asked Chris.

"She comes this afternoon, Maria answered. "They stay at Uncle John's house since he and Aunt Helen will be with Niko, who graduates from college in Thessaloniki. I guess maybe they are the only ones from the village who will miss the wedding."

"Can't wait to see them too," Chris explained to Erika. "Sophia is my other sister, who lives with her husband Constantine, in Athens. Been a while since I've seen them also."

"So don't stay away so long," Maria admonished. "Come see your family more often."

"I promise to do better," Chris said. "But for now, we're gone again. Going to take Erika hiking up to Ayios Thanassios, where you can see all the way to tomorrow. We'll be back late this afternoon." He got up and walked to his sister standing at the sink. "What's in the fridge we can take with us to munch on during the day?"

"Whatever you like," Maria said. "Is plenty left from last night. Lamb, potatoes, everything. Take as much as you want."

"That's pretty serious stuff for a hike," Erika suggested. "I'm still stuffed from the feast last night."

"How about some bread, hard cheese, and some olives," Chris asked. "We can be real ethnic."

"Sounds great," Erika said. "Even that will be a lot. Especially if we're having another big meal tonight."

Maria took a plastic bag from the pantry and placed a whole loaf of bread in it. She wrapped a chunk of cheese in aluminum foil and dropped it along with some olives into the sack. Browsing through the refrigerator, she took a large bottle of cold water and handed it to Chris. He grabbed a couple of apples from a big bowl on the table and tossed them to Erika, who placed them in the bag. Chris then put the entire bag into his backpack.

"Why don't you let me carry some of that?" Erika asked. "I'll be eating too, you know."

"No, you've got your camera gear to lug around," he replied. "I'll carry the groceries."

"Is part of the Greek male ego," Maria said. "Don't worry, Erika, it makes him feel good."

"That's it," Chris smiled. "We're outta here. See you tonight." He kissed his sister and she made a kicking motion as if booting him from her kitchen.

"*Me to kalo,*" she said. "Erika, I hope you enjoy your day."

"I'm sure I will, Maria," Erika said. "We'll see you tonight."

Chris and Erika shouldered their packs and left the kitchen, stopping for a moment on the porch to drink in the day. The sun had already brushed away the coolness of the morning, and was beginning its climb across another crystal blue sky. A slight breeze kept the temperature a delightfully dry seventy-something.

Walking through the village, they stopped several times to chat with some of the neighbors. Most were elderly women sweeping their patios or sprinkling water from cans and pitchers onto their flowers. Each knew Chris, and he went through the obligatory introductions of Erika that by now were becoming routine.

Passing the coffee house, Chris waved at several groups of old men huddled around dilapidated card tables set underneath a giant elm tree in the courtyard. Each was nursing a demitasse of Greek coffee as part of their daily ritual of meeting at the *kafenion* and discussing everything from the weather to their health to world events. Chris pointed out that the locals felt that the elm tree was probably over 200 years old, as stories continued to circulate about great-grandparents and great great-grandparents who sat under its boughs as children.

"Legend has it," Chris explained, "that if you kiss a girl under this tree you both will return someday to Stavroula. It's kind of like the village's own Trevi Fountain tradition with a Greek adaptation."

"Is it really a village legend," Erika asked, "or part of the Chris Pappas embellishment?"

"You don't think I'd make up something like that, do you?" asked Chris, seeming astonished. "Jeez," he said, "whatever happened to trust?"

"Yeah, right. I told you, Greek boy, I've been around the block a few times myself. This is not my first rodeo."

They laughed and continued on the road that led past a few more whitewashed houses covered in flaming bougainvillea. In a few minutes they reached the end of the pavement, and the road continued as a dirt track toward a peak that rose another 500 feet or so above the fields of olive trees that surrounded the cluster of homes. A smattering of small but neat farm homes dotted both sides of the road for another half mile. After that, the road snaked away into the distance across a series of broken hills, and became steeper as it climbed into the mountains.

Chris explained that their hike would carry them into the mountains, where only a few herdsmen watched over their sheep and goats grazing in the hills. There would be very little human presence until they reached the other small villages that were connected by the single mountain road. Erika delighted at the way the lilting names of the tiny communities—Mari, Kounoupia, Peleta, Palihori—seemed to roll off Chris's tongue. Like Stavroula, most had been there for centuries and were almost abandoned except for the old timers and the summer vacationers escaping the big city heat and noise.

She noticed that not much grew in the relatively flat fields surrounding the village. The hardy olive trees were about the only things that could survive the rocky soil and withstand the dry, hot days that stretched from May until October. Almost every home in the village, however, and each of the farmhouses at the edge of town, had a well-built grape arbor. The vines were lovingly tended, and each family took great pride in the quality of their own white and red grapes. Most yielded enough fruit to enable their owners to make several gallons of wine, the quality of which was debated for hours by the old men in the coffee house. Each one extolled the virtues of his own signature vintage.

Chris pointed out a number of silent reminders of the agriculture that had been planted in the area years ago. Wheat had done surprisingly well on the plateau in the past, and was an important crop until the more readily available loaf bread became popular in the stores and among the local people. It was also much cheaper than the traditional process of the farmers growing, harvesting, milling, and grinding the wheat themselves to make their own flour. Water for irrigation was also an expensive and unreliable commodity here in the mountains.

Erika was curious as to the purpose of the large, flat, circular areas that dotted the landscape. Chris stopped at several, and explained how the farmers in the old days harnessed a mule to a long wooden pole and walked the animal for hours around the circular enclosure to grind the wheat. There were no rivers here whose power they could harness to operate a gristmill, nor were there the constant ocean breezes to power the windmills that performed these operations on the islands. Here, the mule served not only as the primary means of transportation before most families were able to purchase cars, but also as the beast of burden in grinding wheat and carrying heavy loads. Life had been hard here.

Chapter Ten

The road grew increasingly steep and the countryside became noticeably more barren as they climbed further into the hills and left the few farmhouses behind. The small scrub brush and a few patches of weeds were the only vegetation visible all the way up the side of the peak rising before them. Other than a few birds flitting among the bushes there were no signs of animal life at all.

Erika was curious as to what message was printed on the small wooden signs that dotted the side of the road at about quarter mile intervals.

"What are they saying?" she asked.

"It means 'no hunting'," Chris answered.

"What in the world would anyone hunt up here? This land doesn't look like it would support any wildlife. No water, and looks like very little to eat."

"Actually, there are a lot of rabbits around," Chris said. "If we drove up here at night to see the little chapel on the summit, you'd see them running all over the place."

"Is that where we're going," Erika asked, pointing to a tiny whitewashed structure perched on the summit of the peak.

"No, the trail to the chapel turns off this road just ahead. We'll continue on to the next ridge to a much older little chapel that overlooks the bay. It's really a pretty sight."

"Will there be time to see this one too while we're here? I'd really like to take some shots of the valley from up there with the village situated in the center. And some shots of the church up there too."

"Not a problem. I thought we'd go one afternoon towards sunset when you'd have the best light. The chapel itself is open so you can shoot inside, too."

"Is it very old?"

"No, no. The villagers built it in the 1950s and dedicated it to the prophet Elia. Most Orthodox churches and cathedrals honor some saint or another. The village comes up here once a year for a service to commemorate the man's feast day, and the rest of the time it is hardly ever visited."

As they rounded a bend in the road, a narrow rocky trail turned off to the left and wound its way in a series of steep switchbacks toward the chapel on the summit.

"This is where you turn to go up there," Chris said. "We'll stay on this road."

Both Chris and Erika were breathing deeply as the road continued to climb. Stopping for a breath, Chris pointed out several small villages tucked away in the mountains far in the distance. None appeared to be any larger than Stavroula, and each seemed to be a tiny oasis on the barren landscape. Continuing on, they crested a hill and came into view of what appeared to be a large encampment.

"What in the world is all that?" Erika asked.

"They're gypsies," Chris answered. "I didn't realize any of them still camped up here in the mountains. Most of them stay down near Leonidion and follow the available work on the farms down there. Considering their reputation for thievery, however, most people want them camped away from the towns."

There were about a dozen vehicles in the camp. Most were rusting travel trailers, decrepit conversion vans, and old trucks jury-rigged into some type of mobile habitation. A few awnings were strung between some of them, and several small cook fires were being tended by women. A handful of ragged children and yelping dogs chased each other through the camp. There were no men in sight except for a few older ones who lounged in the shade of the awnings.

Chris explained that other than their substitution of trailers for the horses and wagons they traveled in years ago, their lives hadn't changed much over the past couple of centuries. They still roamed the Balkans and southern Europe in search of seasonal work. After the local crops were harvested, they moved on to other areas.

Chris and Erika sat on a large rock overlooking the camp while Chris recounted the wandering lifestyle of the gypsies. Suddenly they became aware of a melody drifting to them on the wind from a girl in the camp singing while she was hanging laundry on a clothesline. They listened in silence as the crystal clear notes of the song began to captivate them. The girl sang as if she were performing before a packed house at Carnegie Hall—a passionate, soulful melody that resonated through the hills. She continued her work and her song, oblivious to the presence of anyone around her. Hers was the only sound in the world at that time. Not a bird was singing, and even the dogs had stopped barking. The people in the camp carried on as if nothing was happening. Chris and Erika, however, were mesmerized. They sat in hypnotic silence as the girl sang with a passion that comes only from the heart. When she finished hanging the wet clothes on the line, she carried her basket back inside her trailer. The hills again fell silent.

"That was the most beautiful song I have ever heard," Erika remarked quietly, as if not to disturb the silence.

"If I had a tape of that I could forget about being a starving writer," Chris said.

"Seriously," Erika said, "that was the most haunting melody I believe I have ever listened to. And it just sort of floated over the camp all the way to us up here. Do you have any idea what she was saying?"

"Well, I'd love to be able to manufacture a story for you of a tragic love song sung by a beautiful gypsy girl, but I can't. Most of the gypsies come down from Eastern Europe, and over the years have learned to speak only a smattering of Greek. That really was incredible, though, wasn't it?"

"Chris, I don't know if I'll ever forget that song," Erika said, "and the setting where we heard it. That was a true performance."

Chris looked at her. The song had captivated Erika, and she had totally captivated him. He had seen several sides of her—the consummate professional, the enthusiastic tourist, the playful tease, and now, the romantic. She's really got it all, he thought.

Resuming their hike, they came upon a teenage boy and a dog watching over a herd of goats. The dog began a lively session of barking and moving menacingly until the boy yelled at him and threatened him with his stick. Chris knew the boy and they shook hands and talked, but it was apparent that he was not an old close friend like the many they had met in the village. He wore a faded Nike T-shirt and a pair of jeans that were obviously hand-me-downs from a much fatter, older brother. A piece of rope kept the baggy pants around his small waist. His shoes were old, worn out brogans that he wore with no socks.

Chris and Erika shared the shade of the boy's tree, and talked as the dog kept the goats from wandering too far. The boy declined their offer of some water, producing his own bottle in a tattered plastic bag. He looked with great interest, however, at the couple's backpacks with their state-of-the-art zippers, snaps, Velcro closures, and multi-compartments. Erika found herself wishing she had another one tucked away in her luggage so that she could give this one to the boy. She felt sure it would certainly become one of his most prized possessions.

Moving on, they followed the road further into the mountains until they reached a steep, narrow goat trail that struck off to the left through the brush. They followed the trail as it snaked up the side of a steep cliff that had a series of false summits. Even the scrub brush vanished as they got higher into the rocks. They stopped several times to breathe as the trail became even steeper.

"I guess this is why these people look so lean and fit," Erika said, in between deep breaths at a rest stop.

"Even the goats would have a tough time here," Chris panted. "But it's not much further now."

"What is it we're looking for?" Erika asked.

"It's a tiny little church," Chris said. "The villagers say it's about 200 years old. But close by are the ruins of two medieval churches that go back about 500 years. "They've pretty much crumbled and fallen now, but you can still see some of the walls and pieces of frescoes in the ruins. It's an interesting place, and the views are fantastic."

"You should be on the local tourism board promoting this area," Erika said. "You really feel all this, don't you? I mean the history, the people, all of it."

"I guess I do," Chris said, looking out over the wild hills. "A lot of people, even many who live here, just see a lot of rocks. But if these rocks could talk…" His voice trailed off as memories of many happy hours hiking these hills with his father engulfed him.

"But I don't want to live here," he said. "I'd love to be financially secure enough to spend a month or two here each year. But then I'm ready to go back to the States. That's home for me now. I've traveled to a million places around the world, and I've enjoyed most of them, but they all look better to me in the rear-view mirror. I don't want to live anywhere but the States."

"Are we so perfect there?"

"No, far from it. But we're way ahead of anything else I've seen."

"Could you live somewhere other than in good ol' Alabama?" she asked playfully.

Interesting question, he thought. Why would she ask that?

"I think I could. I guess it would depend on what the attraction was."

Erika shouldered her pack with a smile, and continued the climb. Chris watched her for a second. Then he picked up his pack and followed.

They finally reached a long ridgeline that was the crest of the mountain. The azure blue Aegean lay shimmering in the distance under the midday sun. The trail on the ridge was very narrow with a steep drop off on both sides. It fell away precipitously on the right hand side almost 500 feet before it became a more gradual descent through a forest of olive trees to a village that hugged the shoreline. From this vantage point, the village seemed to be the eastern terminus of the road leading out of Leonidion. The orange of the barren, rocky cliffs gave way to the patches of dusty brown trees and brush on the lower slopes and finally to the lush green of the irrigated fields around Leonidion and the cobalt blue of the ocean. Waves of color from the summit to the sea.

"Simply gorgeous," Erika said. "It would take the breath away even if we weren't huffing and puffing from the climb. What is the name of the little seaside town?"

"It's called Poulithra," Chris said. "Just a few houses and farms and a handful of coffee houses and restaurants. They've built a couple of very nice little hotels there in recent years. It's a great place to spend a few days. The beach is nice, and it's really quiet and peaceful there. Look over here."

He walked a short distance to a series of crumbling ruins that appeared to have been a small house. Only the outer stone walls remained.

"This was an old church during the Byzantine days," he explained. "The old folks tell me that it was supposedly built back in the 1400s. You can even see some traces of the frescoes that were painted on the walls."

They prowled through the ruins, and Erika became fascinated with the tiny traces of wall paintings they found. She took roll after roll of film of the ruins, close-up shots of the frescoes, and scenics with the mountain ranges and the ocean in the distance. Chris sat among the rocks and watched her load, re-load, and change lenses and filters.

"I can't imagine the faith these people must have had to construct something like this in such a remote spot," she said, finally taking a break. "These things must have been beautiful in their day."

"Beautiful in their miniature size and simplicity," Chris said. "They say that the villages around here in those days were just a handful of people, so their churches were tiny too. Any of the people who made the long pilgrimage to the big cities like Athens to see the giant cathedrals there must have really been dazzled."

They walked a little further to the ruins of another small chapel that was very similar to the first. Like the other, it had no roof. Only a few exterior stone walls were intact. After examining the walls and the rocks for traces of frescoes, they leaned back against the rocks and gazed at the sky.

"I bet this would be an incredible place to watch the night sky," Erika mused. Lying in the rocks with her hands clasped behind her head, she appeared to Chris to be lost in the moment. Lying next to her, gazing skyward, he allowed his mind to imagine them in that exact spot on a cloudless night staring at a billion stars twinkling against a black velvet sky. Her laughter snapped him out of his daydream.

"What is it?" he asked.

"Just seems so strange that just a three-hour drive from here is the loud, hectic, noisy confusion of millions of people in Athens." She looked at Chris. "I can see how this place holds your heart," she said. "The beauty, the history, the tranquility, all of it would grow on someone. Especially if your roots were here."

"It's got it all," Chris said. "Feels like you're on another planet. I'll be honest with you, though. I've been here a zillion times, but I don't think I have ever enjoyed it as much."

She looked at him. "I'm flattered," she said, "but I wonder if you tell every woman you take up here the same thing?"

Chris smiled at her. "It really is a great place for lines, isn't it," he laughed. "But no, really, you set all this off. I'm glad you're here." He tousled her hair as he got up, and she watched him walk away.

He turned around. "The tour is leaving, aren't you coming?" he asked.

"Oh yeah," she said, "just trying to figure all this out."

They resumed walking the ridgeline, and came to the church of Ayios Thanassios. The tiny whitewashed structure, dazzling in the midday sunlight, was at the exact edge of a cliff that dropped almost 800 feet to the cluster of hotels, restaurants, and coffee houses at the water's edge. A large bell was hung over the small patio that surrounded the entrance to the church. Chris gave the bell a loud ring, and they both smiled as the gong reverberated across the hills.

"Now the people down below know that someone has made the climb up here," he said. "Let me show you the inside."

They entered the church, and waited a few seconds while their eyes adjusted from the brilliance outside to the darkened interior. Chris pointed out the icons of various saints on the walls and the crucifix and other religious symbols on the altar. He lit a candle, placed it in a candlestick near the altar, and dropped some money in a box near the door. Erika carefully studied each of the objects in the room. After receiving assurance from Chris that photography would not offend any of the somber figures gazing impassively at them from their picture frames, she proceeded to snap a roll of film of the interior.

Returning outside, they found a shady spot on the patio, and spread out the lunch they had brought. The fresh bread, cheese, and olives were just enough to fuel their return hike without being too filling.

After extinguishing the candle he had lit by the altar, Chris crossed himself and closed the door to the church. He packed up the remnants of their lunch while Erika snapped a few photographs of the harbor dotted with fishing boats below them.

"Let's do this," she suggested. She placed her camera on a low stone wall and joined Chris near the bell at the edge of the railing. "I'll set the time exposure, and we'll get a shot of us together."

Chris felt his heart start fluttering again, and he knew it was not a result of the climb. She framed the picture, set the exposure, and ran to him to stand together at the rail. She placed her arm around his waist, and his heart kicked into high gear again at her touch. He put his arm around her shoulder, and they smiled as the Nikon whirred. He never took his eyes off her as she walked back to her camera and placed the gear back into her pack.

"Ready to hike back down?" he asked.

She met his gaze and her eyes were wide. The breeze was rustling her hair. "Not really," she smiled, looking out over the landscape, "but I guess we can't stay up here forever."

"Why not? I've seen worse places."

She was silent for a moment before answering him. That same faraway look that overtook her at Cape Sounion was in her eyes again. She seemed to be slipping away just as she had done at the temple.

After a moment she turned to face him. "Chris," she began, "this is wonderful and I'm having a great time, but I told you the day we met that I had come to Greece for some soul searching. A reality check. This has been an escape for me. It's Never Never Land. Sit for a minute and let me tell you, because I feel like I owe you an explanation."

"You don't owe me any…" he began.

"No, I do," she interrupted. "I realize I slip in and out from time to time, and I want to tell you what it is. Part of it, anyway. You are knocking yourself out trying to entertain me and make sure I am enjoying myself. I feel there is an attraction between us, and I don't know where this might be going, but I need to tell you."

They walked to the patio railing. Chris agonized over what she might be ready to explain to him.

"I told you earlier that I had an older brother," she began. "We were very close. Only a year apart and did everything together. I idolized my big brother, and he was always very protective of me. Dad had served in the Navy during World War II, and, while he didn't make a career of it, he always nudged Bruce towards the military. Bruce, however, had his sights set on being a trial lawyer. Always envisioned a career in the courtroom. Dad would have accepted that, but he made it clear that his first love would be for Bruce to find some high-tech job in the Navy and be a career man. Bruce finally relented. After his first year at USC, he quit and joined the Marines. It was 1967. You can imagine where he went."

"Boot camp and straight to Nam," Chris said.

"Exactly. Mom was distraught, naturally, but Dad was proud as punch. Bruce was in Da Nang for only about two weeks before he was sent up to the DMZ. He was in the country less than a month when he was killed. It tore all of us apart. It was like a part of me had died along with him. Mom never said anything, but we could tell that she blamed Dad for driving Bruce to pursue something on which he really did not have his heart set. Something that got him killed. Their lives together changed. They played pretend for a few years, but finally they divorced. I hated the war, the military, and everything associated with that time. It took my only brother from me, and it caused our family to disintegrate. Think how many times across the United States that scene was repeated.

"During my senior year of college, I met a man at an anti-war rally. He had served with the First Air Cavalry Division when they were first deployed to Vietnam in 1965, and lost the use of both of his legs in the fighting in the Ia Drang Valley."

"I read a lot about what happened there," Chris said. "I shipped over in 1969, so it was about four years before me, but it set the tone for the way the war was fought. The Ia Drang was a real meat grinder from what I heard. Hardcore NVA troops, just like what we were up against where I was."

"Well, we got to be very close with the protests we were organizing and the rallies we attended. We spent a lot of time together, and a few years later, we married. His being in a wheelchair never figured into any of it. I just saw him as the personification of the passion that I held for getting out of Southeast Asia. On top of everything else, he was an attorney. My parents never really cared much for him, but the family had drifted so far apart by then that it didn't really matter. We talked with them regularly and visited once in a while, but there was no closeness. Our marriage was okay, I guess, but after America pulled out of Vietnam, we sort of cooled down ourselves. He entered into a period of self-pity that led to problems with alcohol. When he was drinking, he was verbally abusive. I tried everything to reach him—marriage counseling, talking to a priest, relocating, reaching out to him in any way I could. We just kept drifting further apart. The last few years, the marriage was in name only. He had his life, and I had mine. Any time we spent together usually ended in his drinking and destroying me emotionally. He always accused me of going out on him because he was confined to his wheelchair. I felt that he really hated me and resented the fact that I had two good legs while he had given his for a lost cause. It got worse and worse. My only outlet was to immerse myself in my work and try to forget about home life. I did what I needed to do to keep the house running, but just kept to myself mostly. He would get really violent whenever I brought up the subject of leaving him.

"Any time I brought up the subject of divorce, he would always hit me with the guilt trip of bailing out on him just because he was crippled. Finally, it just got to be too much to take. I told him that no one should ever have to live the kind of misery we had been enduring. I contacted a lawyer, and began dissolving the marriage. That's why I fade in and out when something pushes the button. Anything that brings back a memory of what caused me to lose my brother, my mother, my father and now my husband, just knocks me down. You must have gone through some of the same kind of flashbacks from being in combat, didn't you?"

"Everybody who pulled a trigger went through that," Chris said quietly. "You never get over something like that. You just learn to live with it. But the counselors that talked to us stressed how important it was to go on. If you don't, it consumes you. It was incredibly difficult in our case because we came home to a country that had turned its back on us. We symbolized everything that was wrong with Washington, the military, everything. But life goes on and you have to work through it. The guys who couldn't or didn't became statistics themselves. Probably as many Vietnam vets committed suicide as died during the war. Anyway, all that's behind us now. Every day is a new page."

"I finally realized that," she said. "I have been in the midst of a really tough divorce, and have been an emotional wreck for some time. When I finally accepted the course it was taking, I built the traditional wall and have felt somewhat secure behind it. I feel like you might be making a crack in it, though, and it scares me. I don't know if that's good or bad at this time. I'm not sure if I'm ready for that. You've been a perfect gentleman, but the more time we spend together and the more I am around you, I feel like I might be getting into something that I may not be able to handle. Does all that make any sense?"

"Sure it does, but now I want you to listen to me. It's been obvious to everyone else and I know it's obvious to you that I've been starry eyed since I met you. But I don't want you to feel at all uncomfortable about being here or with me or anything else. Let's enjoy the moment, and I promise to do my best not to look like the lovesick teenager and leave as much of your wall intact as you like. Then whatever happens will happen. I appreciate you letting me know the situation. I didn't know if it was something I was doing or…"

"It's nothing you are doing," she interjected. "Really, it's wonderful being here and seeing all this. And I am really looking forward to the parties and the people. But that's part of what has been on my mind, and I wanted you to know. Maybe we'll get to the rest later."

"That's fair enough," he said. "Why don't we cruise on back down and get ready to do some more of the family thing at the wedding?"

He offered her his hand and she took it. They stood facing each other for a second, their eyes locked in an embrace. He flashed his trademark smile, and turned to lead her back down the trail.

Chapter Eleven

The hike back down the mountain was for Chris even more pleasant than the ascent, as Erika had finally shed some light on what was weighing so heavily on her mind. She had intimated that there could be a bit more information forthcoming, but he felt no need to press her on the subject. The fact that she was enjoying herself so completely was elation enough for him. She seemed finally to be opening up.

The tinkling of distant bells indicated that the goatherd they had encountered earlier had nudged his ruminants to lower fields as the afternoon sun began to wane. And the gypsy camp was as silent as a tomb with even the dogs enjoying their late afternoon siestas in the shade.

When Chris and Erika arrived at Chris's sister's house, they found that the family had already left for the church and the much-anticipated matrimonial union of Andreas and Eleni.

"We're not running late are we?" Erika asked.

"No, no," Chris replied. "Ted and Maria and the girls needed to be at the church early because the girls are in the wedding, and they'll be assisting Eleni with whatever it is that brides need to do before they walk down the aisle. We've got plenty of time. You need any help finding anything or figuring out the secrets to your shower?"

Erika laughed. "No," she said. "Took me a few minutes yesterday, but I finally broke the code."

"Great. I'll start getting ready too. Meet you on the porch when you're finished."

Erika retreated to her bathroom, and Chris decided to let her finish her shower before turning on the water in his. Ted had been working on improving the water pressure in the home's plumbing system, but it still slowed to a faint trickle if both showers ran simultaneously. He removed a dark blue jacket and a pair of khaki slacks from the closet and placed them on his bed.

He also rummaged through two large boxes to find the dress shoes that he kept at Maria's house for church and other special occasions.

Walking down the hall to pick up some towels, he heard the soft humming of a tune emanating from Erika's bathroom. It suddenly struck him that she was humming the song that they had heard the gypsy girl singing earlier that day. He stopped in his tracks to listen, amazed that even though she didn't have any of the words, she was recreating the melody almost exactly.

Now that's an ear for music, he thought. She hears the song once and picks it up immediately.

"Sing some more," Chris called out to Erika. "That's great!"

He could hear Erika laughing in the shower. "You don't want to hear me sing," she answered. "Only girl in our high school who didn't get a second tryout with the glee club. Devastating to a fifteen-year-old."

Chris shaved, showered, dressed, and walked down the hall to the kitchen.

"How are you coming along?" he called out again to Erika as he walked by her room. "Don't need any help, do you?"

"I'm managing quite well, thank you," Erika laughed. "Be there in just a couple of minutes."

Chris smiled and went into the kitchen, where he liberated one of Ted's Amstel beers from the refrigerator. He walked out onto the porch and kicked back in a chair with his feet propped up on the railing.

Good thing Maria's not here, he mused. He knew she would shoo his size twelve feet off her whitewashed railing with the same good-natured scolding she had used on him for years and which he had come to enjoy.

God, it's great to be right here at this particular moment in time, he thought. Beautiful sunset coming up, cold beer going down, and getting ready to step out with someone who has lit a fire in me unlike anything I've ever known before. Life doesn't get much better than this.

Halfway through his Amstel, the door opened and Erika walked onto the porch. If he thought she looked striking last night at the dinner party, she was positively stunning right now.

She was wearing a sleeveless yellow cotton dress that wafted about her as she turned and pivoted for him in order to get the full effect. Her shoulders and arms were slightly bronzed from the afternoon in the sun. A black belt accentuated her small waist while her shapely legs tapered into a pair of low heeled white shoes. She held a white purse and white shawl in her hands. It was the first time that he had seen her really dressed up since they had met, and the effect was overwhelming.

"This look okay?" she asked demurely.

He looked at her for a moment before answering. Realizing how foolish he must look sitting there awestruck, he finally found words.

"Positively stunning," he stammered.

Erika smiled. "You sure know how to give a girl a compliment, Greek boy," she said.

"Only problem is that you'll probably steal the poor bride's thunder," he added.

"Seriously, now," she admonished, "it's not too short, is it? And don't I need a hat or something to cover the head in your church?"

"No and no on both counts," Chris said. "You look perfect." He stood up and took her hand. "Devastating is probably more appropriate."

She smiled and looked deep into his eyes. There was much she needed to tell him and, in time, she would. But right now she felt like Cinderella going to the ball. A truly magical moment.

"You're sweet," she said. "Thanks for making me feel so special. This all comes at a time in my life when I really need a lift."

"Would you like a beer or a glass of wine before we go?" Chris asked.

"No thanks. I'm sure there will be plenty of both at the reception, and I need to pace myself."

He took a long pull from his beer and placed the bottle on the table.

"We're set, then," he said. "Let's go."

Chris offered Erika his arm, and they descended the steps and walked through the courtyard into the narrow lane. He felt a warm glow from having downed the Amstel so quickly, but he knew that Erika's intoxicating nearness was the real reason for his heart palpitations.

He pointed out some of the homes in the village to Erika as they walked arm in arm to the church. Many were crumbling ruins that had been unoccupied for years and were held together only by gravity and the familiarity of the old stones with each other. Others were bright, tidy little whitewashed stucco structures awash in brilliant bougainvillea and climbing roses. He identified the family that lived in this house, how long that one had been empty, and how the son who grew up in another was now working in Athens. They noticed several other couples, mostly old men leaning on weathered walking canes, being led slowly by their wives, wending their way to the church.

The sun had slipped behind the mountains, and the twilight brought with it a slight breeze and a silence that trickled over the landscape. The same earthy smell that permeates all rural settings hung enticingly in the air.

Arriving at the church, they encountered several couples who were huddled around the entrance. The men were smoking their last cigarettes before beginning their enforced abstinence for the next forty-five or so minutes that the Greek Orthodox wedding ceremony would require. Chris offered each a perfunctory greeting and led Erika inside, where he went through the ritual of lighting a candle and crossing himself in front of an icon. They then walked to a spot near the front where Erika could best view the ceremony. Erika noticed Uncle Spiro and Aunt Alexandra standing near to them on the right. The old man, regal in his dark suit and dazzling white hair, turned to wink and flash her a welcoming smile that exploded across his face.

She was surprised that there were no pews in the church. Except for a handful of the oldest guests who were seated in wooden folding chairs placed against both walls, the entire congregation of about 100 people was standing. The priest in his flowing vestments was readying several objects around a table in front of the altar. Byzantine-style paintings of four of the church's saints graced an equal number of huge doors on either side of the altar, and opened into the inner sanctuary where only the priest was allowed to go. An assortment of somber-faced angels, saints, and ancient clerics of the early Orthodox Church gazed intently at the entire congregation from their gilded frames that hung from the walls. A huge stained glass window was diffusing the lingering twilight into multi-hued patterns on the floor. Two white-haired gentlemen, each sporting flowing handlebar mustaches, stood before a chanter's lectern off to the side, and flipped through hymnals and prayer books in preparation for their roles in the service. Several candlesticks on both sides of the priest's table held dozens of lit tapers that cast their soft glow over the entire scene.

Erika thought that each element in the mix combined perfectly to paint a portrait taken directly from the Middle Ages. She also felt strangely alien. Over the last few years, she had spent little time in churches. It wasn't that she had anything against organized religion. It was just that she never felt that it held much for her. Perhaps her lack of a strong faith was another void that she felt existed in her life.

Ted and Maria were standing three rows ahead of Chris and Erika on the left side of the congregation, where the groom's family and friends were located. When all was ready, the priest came forward and stood at the table, signaling that the ceremony was about to begin.

The groom's parents and grandparents proceeded down the aisle and took their places at the front of the congregation on the right side, followed by the bride's mother, who did the same on the left.

A pianist tucked away in an alcove in the back began playing softly. It reminded Chris of the money that he and the many sons and daughters of Stavroula who now resided in the United States had sent back to the village over the years for various civic improvements. The piano had been a gift to the church from one of his cousins in memory of his father and mother. American money had also helped finance the road that connected Stavroula to Leonidion, and had been the main impetus behind the new water system that ended the villagers' reliance on individual wells. Even this church was built primarily with funds sent by families who had grown up in the village and immigrated to America in search of a better life. That pipeline helped sustain an important bond between these people and the land of their birth.

Andreas and his best man emerged from a side doorway and stood at the bottom of the three steps leading up to the priest and his altar. The bridesmaids, including Maria's daughters, began their slow individual walks down the aisle and ascended the steps to stand on either side of the priest. Each girl was radiant in an off-the-shoulder lavender dress and clutching a small bouquet of white flowers. They were followed by the groom's men, handsome in their dark suits and jet-black hair and mustaches. A young boy who looked to be about eight years old, dressed in his best Sunday jacket, short pants, and knee-length socks walked down the aisle and handed the priest a tray holding the stefana, the two lace crowns connected by a white ribbon that would signify the bonding of the bridal couple. Last to enter were the flower girls, two darling scene stealers in short white dresses, who walked down the aisle strewing rose petals along the path that the bride would walk with her father. After they took their places alongside the bridal party at the altar, the music stopped. The congregation turned slightly towards the entrance, awaiting the appearance of Eleni and her father.

Unlike the traditional march played at weddings in America, the pianist began a melody unknown to Erika, but beautiful in its simplicity. Eleni began her walk down the aisle with her father. Her white wedding dress and gossamer veil appeared even more brilliant contrasted against her black hair and eyes and her olive complexion. Her father cut a handsome figure, head held high, back erect, and chest proudly thrust out in a manner that would please even the toughest drill sergeant. A bit of moisture, however, was evident around his eyes. His arm-in-arm procession down the aisle with Eleni would be their last walk together as a father and his little girl. In a few minutes, she would become the wife of Andreas. She would always be his daughter, but no longer his little girl. Now she would be a married woman. She would also be the woman whom, if the Lord smiled on him, would give him grandchildren to dote over in his twilight years. A little moisture around the eyes was understandable.

Placing his daughter's hand in that of Andreas, Mr.

Papageorgiou kissed Eleni on both cheeks and took his place standing next to his wife. Erika noticed that Mrs. Papageorgiou squeezed her husband's hand, signifying the pride she felt in him for having so successfully completed what is probably the hardest task that a father ever performs.

The service lasted every bit as long as Chris had advised Erika that it would take. He whispered to her an explanation of the various elements of the ceremony, from the exchanging of the vows and the placing of the *stefana* on their heads to the traditional three walks around the priest's table and the Holy Communion that was administered to both bride and groom. After the priest had consecrated the union, there were the requisite kisses from the couple's parents and the bombardment of rice and good wishes on the beaming newlyweds as they made their way out of the church.

As the congregation began filing out of the church, Erika's thoughts drifted to the day when she had exchanged wedding vows in front of a justice of the peace with a man with whom she had planned to spend the rest of her life. She recalled feeling, as certainly as Eleni did right now, that it would last forever. She found herself hoping that the Fates would decree a happier ending for Eleni's marriage than they had meted out to her.

Chapter Twelve

The reception was held in what had evolved into a sort of community building in the village. Stavroula's two coffee houses were too small to accommodate the dinner and dancing that followed the wedding ceremony, and, even had they been larger, did not lend themselves to such an auspicious occasion. After leaving the church, the bridal party and the guests filed across the street into a large room that had been added to the tiny grocery store that served the village.

White tablecloths had been spread over about twenty tables set up inside and decorated with white ribbons and simple place settings for the guests. Several women had spent the afternoon in the room's kitchen, and were loading the fruits of their day's labors onto individual plates that a half-dozen white-shirted young men would serve to the guests. The room was awash in hypnotic aromas of roasting lamb, potatoes, *pastichio*, the meatball *keftethes*, Greek salad, stuffed grape leaves, and a mountain of home-baked bread. A long table was set up to serve as the bar around which guests were already crowding for a glass of wine from a huge barrel mounted on a rack. Two bartenders were kept busy filling wine glasses and opening soft drinks for the younger set. An elevated bandstand held a quartet of musicians about to begin playing the *sirto*, *sirtaki*, and other traditional tunes that would send the revelers onto the dance floor after dinner. The noise and commotion were amplified by the Greeks themselves, each trying to speak louder than the other in a symphony of laughter, conversation, and convivial greetings.

Chris and Erika were standing at the bar when a beaming Uncle Spiro walked over to them.

"*Yiassas, pethia!*" he welcomed them as he took Chris in his customary bear hug and kissed Erika on both cheeks. "How you like the wedding, *koukla*?" he asked Erika.

"It was beautiful, Uncle Spiro," she answered. "They make a

lovely couple."

"Well, *koukla*," he continued with a wink, " the Greeks say that going to a wedding has makings of another. Who knows what happens tomorrow, eh?"

Erika smiled and blushed noticeably.

"Thanks, Uncle Spiro," Chris interjected, laughing. "Guess we'll move on now before you really scare her off. We'll see you at the table."

He whisked Erika away to introduce her to other guests who were gathered in groups around the room staking out their places at various tables for dinner. The musicians had begun their first tunes, turning the already soaring sound level in the room a notch higher.

"Christo!" a voice called out above the din. He and Erika turned to see a woman and man hurrying across the room to throw themselves into Chris's arms. She was almost a clone of Maria, only a little younger. The same height, dark eyes, but noticeably thinner. Her husband also appeared to be young, and was very nattily dressed in a dark suit. He was wearing wire-rimmed glasses that belied his position as a doctor in Athens. "How is my little brother," the woman asked after a shower of kisses, "and who is this with him?"

"Sophia, this is Erika," Chris explained, introducing the two. "Erika, this is my sister, Sophia, and her husband, Constantinos."

"It is a pleasure to meet you both," Erika said, extending her hand. For the first time since arriving in the village, Erika was aware that her offered hand was shaken instead of being given the immediate hugs and kisses that had punctuated each of her other introductions.

"I met Erika in Athens the other day, and invited her to come with me to the village for the wedding," Chris said. "She lives in California."

Sophia and her husband were friendly and charming, but Erika was getting the feeling, again for the first time since her arrival, that she was being sized up. There was definitely not the same warmth and openness from the big city couple that she had found among the people living in Stavroula. She also got the impression that Chris was much closer to his older sister, probably as she had played a more maternal role while he was growing up.

After a round of small talk, the two couples joined Maria and Ted at a table where Uncle Spiro and Aunt Alexandra were already seated. Uncle Spiro arranged the seating at the table and, of course, insisted that Erika be next to him in order that he may offer her his detailed explanation of the events of the evening. With Maria seated at Erika's other side, chiding the old man and rescuing her from his constant stream of conversation, Chris found himself seated across from Ted and Aunt Alexandra. He smiled at Erika and shrugged his shoulders as if to signify his helplessness, and she offered a reassuring smile that she was doing fine and was flattered that each of the relatives was vying for her attention. Maria's daughters were seated at the head table along with the rest of the bridal party, except for the bride and groom, who had yet to make their entrance.

When all the guests were seated, the band's *bouzouki* player approached the microphone and began his short welcoming remarks, all of which were dutifully translated at the table by Uncle Spiro for Erika. When he had finished, the band played a drum roll to which Andreas and Eleni entered the room amid applause, cheers, and tinkling of the glasses. They took their places at the center of the head table next to their parents and Father Nicholas, the diminutive, rosy-cheeked priest of the village.

Father Nicholas, looking every inch the quintessential Orthodox cleric with his flowing gray beard, vestments, and gold cross around his neck, rose and walked to the microphone to deliver a short prayer. The congregation stood as well, crossing themselves at its completion and resuming their animated conversations. The serving party immediately burst forth from the kitchen, bringing individual plates to each of the guests and refilling wine glasses.

Conversation was lively around the table. Maria and Uncle Spiro quizzed Erika as to the hike that afternoon, the adequacy of the picnic lunch, what she thought of the wedding ceremony, and a litany of related questions. Ted related to Chris the weather during the past winter and the success of the harvest of olives and oranges in December and January. The other tables were producing a similar cacophony of noise that was punctuated periodically by the guests tinkling cutlery against their wine glasses—signaling their desire for the bridal couple to kiss—followed by cheers and applause.

The musicians continued playing throughout dinner, and picked up the tempo slightly when the first guests took to the dance floor. The lines of people holding hands or handkerchiefs and stepping lively in their circles around the dance floor drew others into the festivities as the older people sat, talked, and smiled approvingly.

Chris made his way around the table to Erika, who was still surrounded by several people introducing themselves and practicing their English on her.

"You said the other day that you wanted to learn the Greek dances," he smiled, wriggling through the crowd. "Ready to give it a whirl?"

"Absolutely!" she exclaimed. "This has been so much fun. I have met so many wonderful people. I hate to appear rude, though, and walk away."

"As long as it's to the dance floor, all is forgiven," Chris said. "Besides, they'll be out there dancing themselves in a couple of minutes."

Chris latched on to the tail end of one of the lines of dancers, and joined the revelers in the lively *sirtaki* dance. He helped Erika pick up the steps that everyone repeated except for the leader, who whirled, jumped, turned, and gyrated as he led the line around the room. When the song ended everyone clapped. The leader of the band approached the microphone to announce the traditional first dance for the bridal couple alone. The dance floor cleared as Eleni and Andreas rose from their seats at the head table and made their way onto the dance floor. They never took their eyes off each other as they danced to the band's rendition of the theme from *Love Story*. Following their dance, the entire bridal party joined them on the floor for another *syrtaki* led by Eleni's father. After allowing the party their private dance, most of the guests returned to overflow the dance floor with the long dance lines cavorting around the room.

116

During the remainder of the evening, Chris and Erika never sat down. Erika was shepherded through the dance lines by Uncle Spiro, by Ted, and by Maria's daughters. Chris felt privileged when he was periodically able to work his way into the rotation of laughing relatives who tugged at Erika to have her join them in the dancing. Towards the end of the evening, Uncle Spiro sat next to Maria sipping coffee at their table and watching Chris and Erika and the throngs still on the dance floor.

"I can't remember when I see Christo enjoying himself like tonight," the old man said. "This girl, she is very special to him I think."

"He's like little boy, Uncle Spiro," Maria agreed. "You should see him at our house. His feet, they don't touch the ground yet, and he's there for two days now. My little brother sees stars right now."

"How you think she feels?" he asked.

"I'm not so sure," Maria began, "but I think maybe she enjoys him too. Is hard for me to believe they only know each other for four days."

"He look so much now like his papa," the old man sighed. "I wish so much to see him so happy like this. Whole time he's married to his wife, I never had good feeling about things. With this one here is different. I feel good from first time I see them together."

"I hope your feelings are right," Maria said. "Little brother needs a wife now. Time to settle down and have family. Too long he's living on the road like gypsy. Better he has wife now and babies. But how she feels I don't know. We visit a little together, and she seems easy person to talk to. Maybe next few days we talk some more."

Sophia and Constantinos made their way across the room and joined Maria and Uncle Spiro at the table.

"So, Maria, tell me about Christo and his girlfriend," Sophia said.

"Spiro and I talk about that right now," Maria said. "Little brother, he walks in the clouds for two days."

"I see that," Sophia answered, "but this girlfriend, she walks up there too?"

Maria shrugged.

"Seem like she is there too," she said. "Only two days I see them together, but they go on like they know each other long time."

"I just hope little brother does not get hurt. The divorce was hardest thing for him. I think it affected him more even than Vietnam. He was much younger when he was soldier. Bounce back better. Was harder for him the divorce."

"We see what happens," Maria said thoughtfully. "We see."

Chapter Thirteen

When the music finally stopped, the bandleader announced that they would be taking a short break. Chris and Erika joined the rest of the party in clapping for the musicians, and returned to their table.

"I think maybe you two have good time, eh?" Uncle Spiro asked as he rose from the table and motioned Erika to take his chair. "Christo, I think maybe she dances better even than you, eh *koukla*?"

Erika laughed as she wiped her forehead with a handkerchief.

"Thanks, Uncle Spiro, but I don't think so," she said. "This is about as much fun, though, as anybody ever needs to have. The dancing, the music, the people enjoying themselves, everything. It's wonderful. I wish I could get these dance steps down."

"What do you mean?" Chris said. "You did great. They played about four different dances, and you picked up the steps to all of them. I guess the musical ear is another of Erika's talents," he said to Maria.

"I wish," Erika said. "This Greek dancing is definitely a workout."

"I'll get us something cold," Chris said, getting up to go to the bar. "Anybody else need anything while I'm there?"

"No thank you," Maria said. "Nothing for me."

"Or for me," Sophia added.

"Come, Christo," Uncle Spiro said, "I go with you."

"Be right back," Chris said looking at Erika. He broke into a huge smile and backed into a couple standing behind him. The girls laughed as Chris apologized profusely to the man and his wife. He and Uncle Spiro then made their way to the bar.

"My little brother, he don't see or walk so good past two days," Maria smiled at Erika. "I think maybe you have big effect on him."

Erika smiled and blushed.

"He's really been sweet," she said. "All of you have. This has been a wonderful experience. I really didn't know what to expect coming here. You've all made me feel so welcome."

"We do not get to see little brother too often," Sophia related. "It is very nice to see him now, especially so happy like this. How long you stay in Greece?"

"I'll be here for about another week," Erika said. "Chris was so nice to have brought me here for the wedding and the chance to meet all of you. By myself I would have just seen the regular tourist sights. It's been great getting to do so much more."

"Christo, he told you he's married before?" Sophia asked.

Erika looked at her for a moment before answering to try and get a read on her tone.

"Yes," she said. "I've gone through a divorce myself."

"His divorce was very difficult thing for him," Sophia continued. "Take him long time to get back to way he was before. Always laughing, smiling, and making jokes."

Erika again got the feeling that Sophia was sizing her up in her role as the protective sister. Her tone seemed to imply that they were very concerned to make sure that their brother would not be hurt again.

"I think that divorce is difficult for everyone," she said.

"No more talk of divorce," Maria exclaimed, attempting to break the coolness of the moment. "We celebrate Eleni's wedding now."

"And how better to celebrate a wedding than with wine," Chris interrupted, placing a small tray with four glasses of wine and a pitcher of ice water on the table.

Erika seemed to light up at Chris's return.

"Water for me," she said. "I feel like I could drink the entire pitcher."

"Go ahead," Chris said. "I'll get us another." He sat down beside her. "Having fun?" he asked.

"You mean you can't tell?" Erika beamed. "You Greeks definitely have a lock on the most fun possible at a wedding. And I've really enjoyed visiting with everyone."

"They've really enjoyed you too," he said. "Looks like you've turned every head in the house. I think everybody here has asked who you are."

"Would you stop with that?" Erika scolded. "I don't…"

"What you don't realize or don't appear to be affected by," Chris interrupted, "is the effect you have on people." Then he added with a smile, "Especially me."

She looked long into his eyes, draining every ounce of emotion from him. Uncle Spiro and Aunt Alexandra saved Chris by walking up at that moment.

"*Ella, koukla*," Uncle Spiro said, pulling Erika out of her chair. "Music starts now again. Time for dancing!"

"Uncle Spiro, I think you must have been the person on whose life the film *Zorba the Greek* was based," she laughed. "If Anthony Quinn hadn't played the part, then the role would surely have been yours."

The old man threw his head back and laughed.

"Maybe Anthony Quinn, he plays the role of Spiro when they make the movie on my life too!" he cried.

Grabbing a napkin from the table, Chris smiled at his sisters and joined Erika and Uncle Spiro in one of the dance circles materializing on the dance floor as the band cranked up again.

After almost forty-five minutes and a dozen more dances, Chris led Erika back to their table.

"It's about 1:00 a.m.," he said. "Had enough yet? The party will probably go another hour at least."

"To tell you the truth," she said, "I really am about done in. With the hike this afternoon and the dancing for the past couple of hours, it's been a long day."

"Why don't we start saying our goodbyes?" Chris suggested. "The way the Greeks do it, that will take a while too."

Chris and Erika began the customary round of hugs, kisses, handshakes, and thank yous that accompany all family farewells in Greece. After making the rounds with the entire family, they cornered the bride and groom to offer their best wishes and thanked Eleni's parents for their hospitality.

Walking outside, the cool of the night felt heavenly after the heat generated by the dancing and the stuffiness of the room with its cloud of smoke from dozens of lit cigarettes. It would be a long time, Erika thought, before America's obsession with the smoke-free environment in public places caught on in Greece.

They stepped into the narrow lane and stopped while Erika slipped her shawl around her shoulders. Chris offered her his hand, and they began walking slowly up the hill to Maria's house. The only light was from a sputtering street lamp that dimly lit only a postage stamp-size area outside the church and the coffee house. A short distance away from it, the village was illuminated only by the moon, which, on this night, was spectacular. Chris and Erika stopped to look at the night sky. The moon was a huge, silvery orb in the heavens almost obliterating the stars. It shone so brightly that the cross on the church and the pine and acacia trees in the yard cast long, eerie shadows across the darkened houses and vacant lots in front of them. Not a dog was barking, nor did a breath of wind disturb the silence.

"Wow and wow," Erika whispered. "This is breathtaking. I thought I had seen incredible skies before, but they were just imitations next to this. Did you order all this too?"

"It was requested, but unconfirmed," Chris smiled. "Should be enough light to guide us home." They continued walking. "It reminds me of a song my mother sang to me when I was probably four or five years old. It was about a young child in Greece during the Turkish occupation. The child sang to the moon asking it to shine brightly to light the way to the little school where children went at night to learn the history of Greece. The Turks would not allow the schools to teach anything of Greek history, culture, or religion. To keep their past alive, the Greeks sent their kids to secret learning centers at night. And they succeeded. Even after four centuries of occupation, they kept the light of knowledge burning until their liberation in the 1820s."

"What a beautiful story," Erika said. "I can almost picture a little boy or girl walking along a path through these hills under a moon like this. Sounds like the song has special memories for you."

Chris stopped in the middle of the road and turned to Erika. "The most special part about all this," he said, "is sharing it with you."

Erika looked at him without speaking. The moonlight was reflected in his dancing eyes and the exuberance of his smile, while his curls, tousled from the frenetic dancing, hung exhaustedly, framing his face. She felt herself being pulled closer to him. They locked in an embrace that sent Chris's head spinning while their lips hungrily sought each other. Chris felt her returning his kiss with a passion that seemed to match his own. Finally they pulled apart. Chris felt his knees almost quivering.

"Erika," he began, "this…"

"Shhh," she interrupted, pulling him back to her and placing her head on his shoulder, "don't say anything. Let's just savor this moment. Look at us, kissing like teenagers in the middle of a country road in a deserted village under a gorgeous moon. Just a moment in time."

Neither of them spoke for what seemed like an eternity. The absolute silence of the night engulfed them. Finally, Chris stepped back, still holding both her hands.

"How corny would it sound if I were to say that this has been one of the most memorable days of my life?" he asked.

Erika smiled. "It wouldn't sound corny at all, if it was true," she said.

"Well, you can believe it then. This has been perfect. I don't want it to end."

She looked past him into the night, a faraway glimmer in her eyes.

"We still have a few days here, don't we?" she asked.

"I don't mean that. I mean I want to see you when we leave Greece and go back to the States. I think I am toast."

She smiled and continued holding his hand as she turned to continue their walk.

"We're taking this one day at a time, remember?"

"Yes, I do. But remember this too. I've never been a good poker player. People can read my face as easily as a book. I think it's obvious that I'm cross-eyed over you. Hell, I need to put rocks in my shoes to keep my feet on the ground right now."

Erika laughed and squeezed his hand.

"You're too cute, Greek boy. And all these homespun Southern colloquialisms don't hurt either. Let's just take this slowly and see where it goes. Deal?"

They stopped in front of the gate leading into Maria's courtyard. "Deal," he said. They locked again in another fiery embrace. Chris could feel her breathing quicken as he placed his hands around the small of her back and pulled her tightly against him. His own breath kept pace as she dug her fingers into his shoulders and down the length of his arms. Chris took a deep breath and stepped back. He felt like his entire face was on fire.

"Guess we better get inside," Erika said. "Don't want to wake everybody."

"Are you kidding?" Chris laughed. "They're all still at the reception. Probably will be for another hour at least. I told you these Greek affairs run way late. We Americans are the only ones to leave early."

He pulled her to him, and they kissed again. Then he turned and opened the gate. The courtyard had the same phantom-like feel as the village, with the moon shadows bathing Maria's plants and fruit trees. Chris led Erika up the stairs for a final kiss at the doorway.

"Sleep tight, pretty lady," he whispered.

"Thanks for a perfect day, Greek boy," she said. "See you in the morning."

Chris opened the door for Erika and they entered the dark-ened house. She walked down the hallway and stopped at the door to her room. Chris was still in the living room.

"You're not going to bed?" she asked.

"In a minute," Chris said. "Need some water first and then a cold shower. You're pretty deadly in the moonlight."

Erika smiled. "Enough already," she smiled. "I'm trying to behave too. Good night."

"Good night," Chris said.

That's it, he thought, pouring himself a glass of cold water from a pitcher in the refrigerator. I'm cooked. He downed the full glass of water on the way to his bedroom. The cold shower might help, he mused, but he didn't think he'd be sleeping much that night.

Chapter Fourteen

The next ninety-six hours were the most idyllic of Chris's life. The four days that he and Erika spent in the village were the perfect combination of exciting exploration of his favorite mountains and laid-back interludes of quiet relaxation. Even the weather smiled on them. Each of the dry, warm days featured the cloudless, sun-kissed Mediterranean blue sky of the travel brochures, while the nights were cool enough for a fire in the clay firepits in the flower-strewn courtyard of Maria's home.

Chris relished the opportunity to show Erika each of the historic and picturesque sights in the area. A full day was devoted to hiking and climbing along the difficult twelve-mile trail from the village to the ninth-century monastery of Elona. Erika was overwhelmed by the fiery setting of the monastery hewn out of a sheer rock cliff hundreds of feet over the valleys and wild mountain passes below. They lit a candle before the ninth-century icon in the chapel, and sipped Turkish coffee with one of the monks who lived at the monastery.

To recuperate from the rigors of their bushwhacking trip through the mountains, they scheduled a day of lounging on the pristine beach at the Plaka just outside Leonidion. The crystal-clear water lapping the shore beckoned them for short dips in the sea, which Erika found to be much saltier than the more familiar Pacific Ocean just blocks away from her home in Newport Beach. It was also infinitely more peaceful. Absent were the hordes of tourists and crowded California boardwalks. During their walks on the beach, they could count on the fingers of one hand the people they encountered.

That evening they dined at a seaside *taverna* where the tables were set up only a stone's throw from the ocean. They feasted on kalamari, Greek salad, and fish caught just that morning by the local fishermen and sold from their boats in the harbor. Gazing into each other's eyes, they raised a glass of ouzo to toast another spectacular sunset and the perfect ending to what was becoming an uninterrupted string of perfect days.

Returning to Maria's house that evening, Erika drifted off to sleep on Chris's shoulder as they stretched out on a lounge chair in the courtyard. He was in heaven. Erika was bubbling, effervescent, and ever ready for any activity during the day, and seemed to melt in his arms at night under the black velvet canopy of stars. He remained motionless for hours for fear of disturbing her sleep and breaking the magnificence of the moment.

He was totally captivated. When she finally awakened, it was almost 3:00 a.m. They kissed breathlessly in the garden before going inside to their bedrooms.

Ted and Maria made certain that Erika experienced every aspect of life in the village. They awakened her one morning at dawn for a visit to Ted's goat pen, where they showed Erika how to milk the animals. Later, Maria had Erika elbow deep in a giant vat of that milk, instructing her in the art of making feta cheese.

Chris watched amusedly as Erika, spattered with flour, joined Maria in preparing loaves of bread for baking in the outdoor oven. He also became the photographer, taking photographs of the two women proudly holding their freshly baked goods on long wooden spatulas near the fire.

They also spent hours roaming Ted's olive groves, showing Erika how the locals used ladders to climb into the trees and shake the olives from the branches when the berries ripened in the winter.

Eager to go back into the mountains, Erika begged Chris for another hike. He led her on another all-day foray into the hills, walking past the tiny villages of Peleta and Houni to the home of Chris's Aunt Margaret in the town of Mari. The tiny, fair-skinned lady in the traditional black dress immediately took to Erika, and delighted in showing her the flowers, grape arbors and fruit trees that surrounded her home. She also served them a mound of Greek-style spaghetti and plates of wild greens in olive oil to revive them after their ten-hour trek through the mountains. Ted drove to Mari in his pickup truck to return the exhausted hikers to Stavroula under another crystal clear night.

One of Erika's favorite excursions was their overnight

camping trip to the overlook at the chapel of the Prophet Elia. Following dinner one evening, Chris and Erika left Maria's house for the six-mile hike up the switchback road to the chapel. Ted and Maria later drove to the chapel to meet them and bring their sleeping bags. Together, they built a fire and uncorked a bottle of wine while watching the sun slip again into the Mediterranean from the terrace outside the tiny chapel. Having forgotten the wine glasses at her home, Maria passed out plastic cups for them to drink from.

"I don't think I could ever tire of seeing that," Erika sighed, looking out at the ocean on one side and at the mountains on the other. "You guys have a real treasure here. This place, the lifestyle, everything. I can't tell you how much I've enjoyed the past few days. It's been absolutely perfect."

"We very glad you like it," Ted said, now more confidently using the little English in his vocabulary. "Maybe you come back soon?"

"She hasn't gone yet," Chris interjected. He looked at Erika. "What's the time frame for you?" he asked. "We really haven't talked much about going back home."

"My flight is in four days," she said.

"How about this, then, as a plan," he began. "We can go back to Athens and spend one night. If we leave here, say, midmorning, it will put us back in Athens by midafternoon. The next day we could drive to Delphi. It's an incredibly scenic trip and one of the most important sites in Greece. Navel of the earth in ancient days, site of the oracle, the whole works. Spend the night and the next day up there, drive back to Athens that evening, fly home the next day. I am scheduled to go back a day later, but I can change my ticket so we could leave the same day. What do you think?"

"Sounds like a great plan," Erika said excitedly. "Delphi is on the tourist trail, and turns up in all the travel literature on Greece that I had with me. Are you sure you're not sick of me yet?"

Chris smiled. "Not by a long shot," he said. "I'm already planning another little adventure. Ever been to Alabama?"

Erika blushed, and Ted and Maria laughed.

"Slow down, little brother," Maria said. "Don't scare this one so quick away. I think maybe we like her very much."

"I love all of you too," Erika said, raising her cup to toast the occasion. "Let's drink to good friends."

"Christo," Maria said, "you have good toast in English for friends, no? I hear you say it one time before. How it goes?"

Chris raised his cup and looked directly at Erika. "There are good ships and wood ships, the ships that sail the sea, but the best ships are friendships and may ours ever be."

"I love that!" Erika said, clinking her cup with those of Maria, Ted and Chris. "Good job, Greek boy," she smiled. "Still haven't run out of clever lines."

"I've only just begun," Chris replied.

"Well, we not beginning, we ending," Maria said rising to leave. "*Pame, Thodori?*" she asked Ted, signaling it was time to go.

Chris followed Ted to the car and removed the two sleeping bags, a couple of pillows, and a flashlight from the trunk. Ted also handed Chris another bottle of wine.

"Maybe for later, eh?" Ted asked.

"Thanks," Chris smiled. "See you in the morning."

Erika and Maria joined them at the car.

"Good night, little brother," Maria said. "If too cold it gets tonight, ring the bell in the chapel and maybe Ted comes pick you up." Then she smiled, "But then again, maybe he don't come pick you up."

"We'll be fine," Chris said, hugging his sister. "Thanks for everything."

Erika hugged Maria and Ted, and stood in the roadway holding Chris's hand as they waved the couple goodbye.

"The temperature is dropping," Chris noted. "Shall we put another log on the fire?"

"Good idea," Erika said. "Can't believe how cool it gets at night after such warm, balmy days."

"Even in July and August we use blankets at night up here in the village," Chris said. "That's why the area is so popular as a summer retreat with the Athens crowd. We can spread our bags by the fire or, if you're too cold, we can sleep inside the chapel. What's your pleasure?"

"Got to be here by the fire," Erika answered. "Couldn't miss this spectacular sky."

"Great," Chris said. "How about some more wine?"

"Why not," Erika smiled. "We're not driving."

Chris emptied the last of the opened bottle into Erika's cup.

"Drinking my brother-in-law's homemade wine from a plastic cup sitting on a rock on top of a mountain getting ready to spend the night in a sleeping bag," he mused. "Maybe not exactly the five-star vacation you had in mind. Can I make it up to you when we get to Athens?"

"You must be kidding," Erika admonished. "This is a million-star hotel. Just look at the sky, and the lights from the village winking at us from below. This couldn't have been scripted any better. I can't tell you how much I have enjoyed this and how appreciative I am for all that you and your family have done. It's been a dream vacation."

"I'm the one who's been living the dream," he said. "I'm cross-eyed over you, and I'm sure you know it. This place in itself is powerful enough for me, and to share it with someone who's had me walking in the clouds for a week has been a fantasy come true. I really mean that."

She snuggled up to him, zipped her parka a little higher, and put her head on his shoulder. Chris wrapped his arms around her and pulled her tightly to him. Erika felt very secure under his strong arm and sensed a peace she had not known in a long time. They sat in silence a long while, gazing hypnotically at the fire and the twinkling lights in the valley.

Erika finally broke the silence. "So what happens now?" she asked almost demurely. "Do these bags zip together?"

Chris turned to look at her. "They do," he said. "What I'm wondering, though, is what's going to happen tomorrow and the day after that and the day after that. Erika, we've known each other for a week. During those seven days, I've learned that I want to pursue this. No one can see into tomorrow or the day after, but I want to see where this will go. You're a much more reserved and analytical person, and that's good because I think and act on emotion."

"I'm that way because I've just gone through a pretty bad time in my life," she interrupted. "I'm cautious and a little slower maybe, but I can tell you I feel a lot of this myself. I'm attracted to you. You are a hopeless romantic, and I am fascinated by that. Maybe it's because I didn't expect that. The irony of it is that I came to Greece looking for just the opposite. I wanted some time alone to sort things out. That hasn't happened. You've complicated a lot of things."

Chris felt his pulse quicken. Despite the chill of the evening, his face was again on fire. He turned to look at her and took her hands in his.

"Listen to me," he said. "I realize that we come from two very different backgrounds and live in two very different worlds. And long distance relationships are difficult. But I'm open to going wherever and doing whatever it takes to see where this leads. Honest."

She smiled and leaned forward to give him a light kiss on the lips.

"That's all a girl could ask for," she said. "Now, what do you have in mind for the sleeping arrangements?"

Chris looked at her for a long moment. The moonglow was highlighting her hair and the wine was dancing ever so gently in her eyes. Could it be just the wine talking?

"Well, for tonight I'd like to zip these bags together and snuggle down and drift off to sleep. I think I've got enough Yankee dollars left to get us a room with a view at your Hilton back in Athens. Maybe even enough left over for a bottle of the finest cheap wine. What do you think?"

"You keep painting pretty good pictures, Greek boy," she smiled. The dazzling whiteness of her smile and the elusive dimples were visible even by the dim firelight. "Guess this wine has helped too."

"Let's turn in, then," Chris said. He rose and zipped the bags together. Erika took off her jacket, kicked off her shoes, and wriggled down into the sleeping bag. Chris stirred the fire until the embers sparked back into a decent flame. He placed another log on the fire before kicking off his shoes and crawling into the bag with Erika. To his great delight, she pulled him to her and kissed him with a passion that made him wonder again whether it was the wine and the setting that had inspired the mood or whether she was genuinely interested. It didn't matter, he thought. His head was spinning out of control. This was heaven.

"I'm looking forward to Athens," she whispered. "Thanks for being so nice."

"Thanks for being here," he said. "Sleep tight."

"Who could possibly sleep with a sky like that going on?" she asked, looking at the heavens.

She kissed him again and turned away while at the same time pressing back against him. He placed his arm around her, and drew her tightly against him. The intoxicating smell of her hair and the feel of her snuggled against him were overpowering. After a few long measured breaths, Erika was sound asleep. Chris smiled. He was the one known for zonking out as soon as his head hit the pillow. Looking past her into the crackling fire, Chris knew that would not be the case tonight, as it seemed it hadn't been since he'd met her.

Chapter Fifteen

"Well, good morning!" Maria said as Chris and Erika walked into the kitchen. "How was the night on the mountain? You freeze all night long?"

"Good morning, Maria," Erika answered. "The night was perfectly lovely. Nice fire, crystal clear sky, and cold enough to make the sleeping bags feel very welcoming. I've been camping before, but that was the first time in my life I've ever slept completely out in the open like that. It was magnificent! A little stiff when I got up this morning, though. The hike back down here helped work out the kinks."

Chris walked over to the sink, where Maria was washing dishes, and kissed her on the cheek.

"Ditto everything she said," he laughed.

"Christo, look at you!" Maria exclaimed. "You look like wild man before you have shower in morning. Better you go now and get cleaned up before you run our Erika away. Then come and I fix you both something to eat."

"Thanks anyway, but I only have time to brush my teeth, and then I'm off to run an errand," Chris said. "Be back shortly."

"Well, where are you off to?" Erika asked, surprised.

"Sorry," he said, "it's a surprise. Maria, is Ted still here or is he down in Leonidion?"

"He goes off with Uncle Spiro early this morning. Why?"

"His truck or Uncle Spiro's?"

"Spiro's. Why?"

"I told you, it's a surprise. I need his truck for about an hour. I'll be back before you even know I'm gone."

"What this surprise business is?" Maria asked.

"I wish I knew too," Erika added. "What are you up to?"

"Not a big deal," Chris laughed, walking down the hall to his bedroom. "Going to grab something, and I'll be back in a flash."

Chris emerged from his bedroom with his backpack, and went

into the bathroom to brush his teeth.

"What do you suppose he's up to?" Erika asked Maria.

"Who knows?" she shrugged. "Baby brother he acts maybe a little strange lately. Here, have a cup of coffee."

She poured Erika a cup of coffee, and gave her a plate with several slices of homemade bread and marmalade.

"Thanks," Erika said, taking a seat at the table. "This looks great. No chance to lose a few pounds here, even with all the hiking and climbing we've been doing."

Chris emerged from the bathroom whistling a tune.

"See you ladies shortly," he said. "Are the keys in the truck?"

"Like always," Maria said. "Go now, mystery boy. We see you later."

Chris waved as he bounded out the door and through the courtyard. Maria and Erika watched from the kitchen window as he walked down the lane, still whistling his tune on his way to the truck.

"Maria, is Chris always this upbeat?" Erika asked. "Seems like he is always happy. I really enjoy his sunny disposition."

Maria smiled. "My baby brother is happiest person I know," she said. "He feels very, how you say, fortunate. He says he is doing the work he loves to do, and enjoys all his friends. He tells me one time that, for him, every day is Christmas. Especially after what he goes through when he was in the army in Vietnam."

Erika grew serious. "That was a terrible time," she said. "A bad time at home, and I can only imagine how horrible it must have been for him and the men over there. Add to that the treatment they received when they came home and it's no wonder that so many were scarred so badly emotionally. Does he ever talk about it?"

"Not so much. He was very lucky. Adjusted very well when he comes home. Very hard for him at first, though. I guess for everybody. It took time, but after a while he's okay. The writing, it has been very good for him. Was like an outlet. Now, he's just like before, always happy and enjoying whatever he does. But I tell you one thing, as happy as he is last few days here with you, I have never seen him."

Erika smiled. "I have really enjoyed it myself," she said. "You all have been just wonderful."

"Forgive me for being nosy sister," Maria said, "but you two plan to see each other again when you go home to America?"

"I think so," Erika said. "I'm still sorting out some leftover business from my divorce. That was part of the reason I wanted to come to Greece in the first place. I think that I am ready now to turn the page and get on with the rest of my life. I don't know how these long distance romances go, but we'll see. I am looking forward to seeing him again."

"I know he is very anxious to see you too," Maria said.

"Has he said anything about it?" Erika asked.

"No need for him to say anything to me," Maria answered. "I know my baby brother very well. I look in his eyes and see stars there. I hope things work out so you get to know each other. Then whatever is meant to be will be."

"I guess so," Erika said. "You Greeks have such a wonderful way of looking at things. I wish life were so simple."

"I think maybe life is simple," Maria added. "Maybe people make it more complicated."

"Maybe you're right," Erika smiled. "Anyway, I'd better shower and start getting my things together. Looks like we'll be heading back to Athens tomorrow morning. Then to Delphi. I'm really looking forward to that. Can I help you with anything here?"

"No, no," Maria chided. "You go ahead and do what you need to do."

Erika finished her coffee and bread and placed the dishes in the sink. Then she went to her room to begin packing for the return trip to Athens. After a quick shower, she found Maria in her courtyard watering her flowers. Erika assisted her in the garden for about an hour when Maria's daughters came by. They asked to take Erika to the old schoolhouse and show her the grounds, and she quickly accepted.

"You be back here by about one o'clock so we have lunch with your father and Christo," she called to the girls as they headed out the gate with Erika in tow.

The girls spent the next hour pointing out the sights in and around the closed school about a block from Maria's home.

Conditioned to seeing schools set in the heart of American cities or in the sprawling suburbs, Erika thought that the tiny building seemed strangely out of place surrounded by small farm homes. Each yard had a fenced area where the goats, chickens, and mules were kept. While the earthy smell unmistakably identified the area as rural, each home was well scrubbed, neat, and tidy. The stone school building appeared to be in good structural condition despite not having been used during the past ten or so years. It was quiet and deserted now, but Erika tried to imagine the scene years ago, when the playground would have been teeming with children laughing and chasing each other and playing volleyball and soccer. The girls explained that the residents had plans to turn the building into a type of community center, but that no work had been done as yet on the project.

When they returned home, Chris and Ted were relaxing on the patio. The table had been set for lunch, and a series of enticing aromas were wafting out of Maria's kitchen.

"Welcome back, ladies," Chris said with a smile.

"Hi there," Erika said, bending down to give Chris a kiss on the cheek. "Hi Ted," she added, giving him the traditional peck on the cheek also.

Chris noted that Erika appeared now to be completely comfortable with the kiss-on-the-cheek greeting where only a few days before she was still offering the hand at meetings and introductions. His heart again shifted gears thinking that maybe she was really getting into this cultural bit and enjoying it.

"Hello to you," Ted replied. "How you are?"

"Had a great morning, thanks," Erika said.

"Heard you've been taking in the sights," Chris said.

"Had a lovely tour of the school and some of the houses in the neighborhood," Erika answered. "Irene and Anna are first-class tour guides."

The two girls giggled. Ted told them in Greek to go inside and wash for lunch and see if their mother needed any help.

"Looks like the sun has really put the Aegean glow on your cheeks," Chris said to Erika. "No hat?"

"I'll put one on this afternoon," she said. "Want to get a little vacation color to take home with me. Can't have you Greeks getting all the suntan. Couldn't catch up with you, though. Guess you have to have the olive oil in the blood to get your color."

"It helps," Chris smiled.

"I'm going to help Maria with lunch," she said. "You guys want anything from inside?"

"We're fine," Chris said. "I think Maria just about has everything ready to go."

"She has done so much," Erika said. "Promise me one thing."

"What's that?"

"Promise me that tonight you'll let me take all of us out to eat in Leonidion. I can't begin to repay all this hospitality, but I really would like to take everyone out for our last night's dinner. Okay?"

"You'll get a fight out of Ted on that, but I'll use all my incredibly persuasive powers to convince him that you've set your mind on it. Won't be a problem. That's very nice of you to offer."

"Are you kidding? After all they've done for me, it's the very least I could do. Tell him, okay?"

Chris translated to Ted the plans that Erika had for the evening. As Chris expected, he protested, but after a few minutes of good-natured bantering, he relented and accepted.

"Thank you very much," he said. "Is very nice of you."

"It's nothing," Erika said. "I'm going to see what I can help Maria with."

Chris and Ted watched her enter the house.

"This one I like very much," Ted said.

Chris smiled. "This one I like very much too," he answered. "In fact, I'm hooked. I'm trying to go slowly, but I really feel that something is happening. I guess we'll see when we get back to the States."

"Lunch is served," Erika announced, easing open the door and emerging again onto the patio with a huge pan of *moussaka*, the macaroni, cheese, and eggplant casserole that had become one of Erika's favorite Greek dishes.

"Can you believe this?" she asked. "Maria remembered what a fuss I made over the *moussaka* we had, and she prepared it for lunch especially for me. I may, however, let each of you have just a little."

"How nice of you," Chris said. "One of my favorites too."

Maria and the girls followed, bringing a large bowl of Greek salad and a pan of oven-baked Greek-style new potatoes. Erika returned into the house to bring a tray of Coca-Colas, two Heinekens, and a pitcher of ice water. Arranging everything on the table, they were finally ready to begin. Erika noticed that Ted, Maria, and the girls crossed themselves in the Orthodox fashion prior to eating.

"*Kali orexe*," Maria said, bidding them a good appetite. They each raised their glasses for a quick clink, and began an enthusiastic assault on each of the items on the table.

When they had finished, Irene and Anna were joined by Chris and Ted in clearing the dishes and returning everything to the kitchen.

"Well, maybe your American custom of men helping in kitchen catches on now in Greece," Maria mused. "Here in Greece, men sit while women clear table and wash dishes. I think maybe this help not so bad."

"The least we could do," Chris said. "What do you think about siesta time now after that huge meal? Maybe get up later when it cools off and take a walk to the old cemetery."

"Sounds like a great idea," Erika said. "Is it far?"

"No, is only maybe one kilometer," Maria said. "Christo, you take Erika later. Maybe I go with you too."

"Great!" Erika interjected. "Afterwards we can all go into town for dinner. My treat, okay?"

"Sounds like a plan," Chris said. "Now I'm doing my imitation of 'Horizontal Man'. A nap will be perfect after the chilly night on the mountain. See you all later."

They all rose, went into the cool haven of the house, and retired to their individual bedrooms for the afternoon nap which is still an integral part of life in Greece. With the exception of a few tourist-oriented businesses, most shops and offices across the country shut down from about one until four in the afternoon, when most of the cruelty has gone out of the sun, and they reopen for business.

A barking dog brought Chris out of what had been a surprisingly deep sleep. No cat nap here, he thought. This was at least a phase-three power slumber session. Stretching and clearing his head, he rolled out of his bed and headed for the bathroom to wash up. He met Erika walking in the same direction.

"Well, I've seen you wake up twice now in the same day," he smiled. "Still look like a magazine cover."

"Hardly," she laughed, "but that was a wonderful nap. I really slept soundly."

"Me too. Go ahead and wash up and we'll get ready to walk to the old cemetery."

She brushed by him and leaned up to give him another kiss on the cheek.

"Thanks," Erika said. "See you in a minute."

Chris walked into the kitchen, thinking that he was noticing an increasing amount of warmth and openness on Erika's part. Was she feeling even a part of what he felt? It's not just my imagination, he mused. She is really offering these little whispers and light kisses on the cheek even when other people are around. Still, he wanted to try and keep all that was happening in context and not let his imagination run away with him and what he hoped was happening.

Ted and Maria were on the patio sipping their afternoon coffee.

"Hello, sleepy boy," Maria said. "Thought maybe you sleep all evening. Maybe you don't sleep so much last night, eh?" she asked with a wry smile.

Chris's face transformed into a huge grin. "I think Erika slept pretty well," he said, "but I spent most of the night just savoring the moment. Incredible time. You going to walk with us to the old cemetery?"

"Sure, unless you maybe want to go alone," Maria said.

"No," Chris smiled. "Come with us. I'm going to wash up and we'll be ready to go."

He walked inside as Erika was leaving the bathroom.

"Your turn," she said. "I'll wait for you on the patio. Where are Maria and Ted?"

"They're on the patio. They're going with us too."

"Great. See you there."

After Chris had brushed his teeth and washed the sleep from

his face, he put on a clean T-shirt and joined the others on the patio. They walked through the courtyard and out the gate into the lane in front of the house. Rather than turning left as they had done when walking to the coffee house, they turned right and walked along a dirt road that led away from the village.

The road was lined by arrow-straight acacia trees and the occasional eucalyptus. Expertly crafted stone fences separated various portions of the fields where crops once grew. The fields now were overgrown with weeds, brambles, and assorted scrub where even the goats would have a hard time finding forage. A few crumbling stone sheds marked the spots where the shepherds once escaped the weather while their flocks had grazed. The quiet was overwhelming.

The road ended in a clearing where a small chapel stood in the midst of a collection of about 100 graves. Each was marked with a small cross or stone tablet, along with photos of the deceased. Ted and Maria pointed out to Erika the story behind several of the markers and the people who occupied the sites. Erika noted the surprising age of each person interred there.

"It seems like everybody here lived into their 80s and even their 90s," she said. "That's an incredible pattern of longevity. What is the secret?"

Ted understood what Erika was asking and wanted to offer an answer, but he asked Chris for help in saying what he wanted to say, though he told him how to phrase his response.

"Is olive oil, red wine, and the walking," Ted said slowly. He looked at Chris for confirmation.

"Seems to be an entire lifestyle thing," Chris said. "Like Ted says, the olive oil in the diet, the red wine, and the exercise they get. Most of these people walked for miles every day, whether tending the animals or moving back and forth between the villages. Must be something to it, since these tombstones show they all lived to be at least octogenarians."

"Wow," Erika said. "Science is just now confirming what they've known for years. That's amazing. And this is such a beautiful setting."

Erika noted that Ted had turned away and was wiping his eyes as he stood over a gravesite. Maria walked over and put her arm around his shoulder.

"That's Ted's mother and father," Chris said. He took her hand and led her to another corner of the cemetery. "That's where my grandfather and grandmother are lying," he said. The same moisture appeared in his eyes. He felt in his pocket for a handkerchief but came up empty. Erika offered him a tissue, and placed her arm around his shoulder in the same manner that Maria had comforted Ted. She sensed that this very special place embodied all that Chris felt for his heritage and the home of his parents. She was surprised to find that the magic of the moment, standing over the graves of people she had never known, was touching even to her.

"The Greeks say *zoi s'emas*," Chris said after a minute. "It means 'life to the living'. But we carry their memories with us forever. They were lives well lived. Those old folks really saw some incredible times."

Chris took Erika's hand and turned back to join Ted and Maria.

"Okay," he said. "Time to go. Always good to come back here for a few moments and shed a tear to keep their memories alive. Now back to the present. Let's get back to the house and get ready for going to dinner. How about Margaret's place in the Plaka?"

"Wherever you like," Maria said. "Is very nice you taking us out."

"Our pleasure," Erika said. "Can't believe we'll be hungry after that wonderful lunch, but I'm sure we'll have an appetite by the time we get there. Chris, what was the Greek term you used a minute ago about life?"

"*Zoi s'emas*," he said.

"Right, *zoi s'emas*" she repeated.

They turned, each walking hand in hand down the road back to the house in the village.

Chapter Sixteen

It seemed to Ted that his bandaged old pickup truck rattled a little less than usual on its journey down the mountain that evening. The smoother ride could have been attributed to the full complement of passengers the truck carried during the five-mile descent from Stavroula to the flat, cultivated fields that had inched their way almost to the beachside restaurants at Plaka.

Ted, Maria, and Erika had wedged themselves into the truck's cab, while Chris, Irene, and Anna rode in the cargo bed. Erika had volunteered to ride in the back with the girls, but Chris's self-proclaimed Southern chivalry had prevailed, pointing out that the truck would likely kick up clouds of dust over the unpaved stretches of the mountain road. The riders in the cab laughed at the squeals and cheers emanating from the trio in the back each time Ted negotiated one of the hairpin turns of the narrow, rock-strewn track.

When they finally arrived in Plaka, the sun had dipped behind the western mountains that rose from the edge of the long, pebbly strand where Chris and Erika had passed such a delightful afternoon just a few days ago. Erika was surprised at how balmy the evening was here at the seaside as opposed to the chill up in the mountains.

The aroma of grilled fish and potatoes fried in olive oil virtually oozed out of the waterfront restaurants and drifted like an aromatic cloud over the entire harbor. They met Uncle Spiro and Aunt Alexandra waiting for them at the seaside *taverna* run by Margaret, another of the family's ubiquitous cousins, and her husband. After a round of hugs and kisses, Margaret led the group to a large table directly on the boardwalk overlooking the harbor. Uncle Spiro again insisted on sitting next to Erika to offer his homespun wisdom and philosophy and his detailed explanation of the merits of Greek cooking. The old man beamed with pride when Erika validated his theories with the scientific community's increasing acceptance of the virtues of olive oil and red wine in the diet. Aunt Alexandra, the epitome of decorum and Old World elegance in her crisp navy blue dress, smiled approvingly from across the table.

The table was soon laden with wine and an assortment of appetizers including fried kalamari, eggplant, and Greek salads. The main course was a delicious fish, broiled and served whole at the table where it was cut into portions by Uncle Spiro.

"Someday, Christo, you learn to do this like me," the old man had proclaimed.

Ted kept the wine glasses filled, which partially accounted for the increasing decibel level of the conversations around the table. By the time the last plate was cleared, the lights were twinkling from the forest of masts rising from the decks of the tired old fishing caiques riding quietly at anchor in the harbor. Everyone had eased back in their chairs, and, after asking permission from Maria and Erika, Ted and Uncle Spiro had lit their ritual after-dinner cigars.

Erika returned from what the others presumed was a visit to the ladies' room, but Chris caught her eye and recognized the actual reason for her trip.

"You went to pay the bill, didn't you?" he asked.

She smiled. "Don't start, now," she admonished. "I told you that this was going to be my treat. I knew that if Margaret brought the bill to the table either you or Ted or Uncle Spiro would have picked it up. It's our last night here, and I wanted this to be my 'thank you' to them for all they've done."

"At least let me split it with you," Chris said.

"No way. You've paid for everything since we met in Sounion. Besides, the whole dinner for all eight of us with drinks and all didn't even come to $100. Other than my hotel bill in Athens, I don't think I've spent any money at all on this trip. How about letting me pick up the tab when we go to Delphi? I've worked with freelancers at the magazine, and I know that most of you guys go the feast or famine route."

"But you know what the nice thing about that is?" Chris asked, sidestepping her question. "It's our own feast or famine. Work out of my home, no commute, no office hours, no schedule, no dress code. I can sit under a tree in my backyard and write my stories. On the other side, we deal with the famine too during the slow times. There's no regular salary or benefits. It's not the right life for everybody, but it's perfect for me."

"It does fit you," Erika said. "Completes the image with the lifestyle."

"I think I'll take that as a compliment," Chris said.

"That's how it was intended," Erika smiled.

Chris sensed that the through-to-the-soul look she was giving him was as intense as his own fixating look into her eyes.

"Hey you two, what is so interesting there?" Uncle Spiro asked.

"*Ella*," Maria chided him. "Let them talk. Maybe they like to have a dinner alone instead of with all of us anytime we go someplace."

"This has been one of the greatest weeks of my life," Erika said. "I want to offer a farewell toast to thank all of you for making me feel so welcome in your home and as part of your family. It has been an experience I will never forget. To good health and good friends!"

They all clinked their glasses at Erika's toast.

"*E seyia*," they all said in Greek.

"Now I've got something I want to give to Erika to commemorate our visit to the village," Chris announced, "and I want to do it with all of you here as I think you will enjoy it too."

"Bravo, Christo!" Uncle Spiro exclaimed. "Show to us what you have."

"Now what's all this?" Erika said. "A surprise on top of everything else?"

Chris rose and began rummaging through his backpack. Anna and Irene ran around to where he was standing, excited about catching a glimpse of the treasure he was about to extract from his bag.

"It's not a big deal," he began, "just a little something to remember the past few days. I hope you like it."

Chris produced a hand-held micro-cassette tape recorder from his pack, and placed it on the table. Then he removed a cassette from a plastic sack.

"You buy her a tape recorder?" Maria asked.

"No," Chris laughed. "This is the recorder I use when I'm interviewing someone for an article. The tape is what I made for her." He looked at Erika as he inserted the cassette into the player and hit the play button.

Immediately the air was awash in the crystal clear notes of the song the gypsy girl was singing on the day that Chris and Erika had passed their camp in the mountains. The sparkling clarity and magnetism of the enchanting melody hypnotized everyone in the *taverna* as completely as it had Chris and Erika on the day of the hike. The table soon attracted cousin Margaret and a crowd of diners and strollers along the boardwalk as each stopped to listen to the aria performed with such passion by the young girl.

Erika's face was that of a child at Christmas. The dazzling smile lit up the dark like the beacon at the head of the entrance to the harbor.

"Unbelievable," she remarked at the conclusion of the song as everyone applauded. "How did you get that recorded?"

"It was when I went off in Ted's truck after we came down from camping at the chapel," he smiled. "I slipped the girl a few bucks, and she felt like she was on stage. Of all the times I've been to the village over the years, being here this time with you has absolutely been the most fantastic. And that song that day in the mountains probably accentuates it more than anything else that has happened. I hope you like it. The recorder is a little old, and there was no place around here to get a new one, so it will have to do until I can get you a replacement."

Erika rose, placed her arms around Chris's neck, and gave him a hug that sent lightning through his body just as it had on each occasion since she first touched him at the Corinth Canal. Everyone at the table applauded and patted Chris on the back.

Erika pulled away and, oblivious to everyone around them, looked directly into his eyes.

"Thank you," she whispered. "It's the loveliest present I could have ever imagined. And I will never play it on another recorder."

Toast, Chris thought. I am toast.

"I'm glad you like it," he said.

Ted, Maria, and the others rose, signaling that it was time to

144

leave. Uncle Spiro told Ted that he was going inside to get the bill from Margaret. Chris interrupted, telling them that Erika had already paid the tab. After much protesting and feigned insulted feelings, they all thanked Erika with additional hugs and kisses.

They decided to stroll to the end of the boardwalk before heading home. The girls ran along ahead, while Ted and Maria followed arm in arm. A few paces behind them were Chris and Erika holding hands. Bringing up the rear were Uncle Spiro and Aunt Alexandra. Chris chuckled.

"What's so funny?" Erika asked.

"This is definitely not a typical Greek scene," Chris said with a smile. "In most Greek families walking like this along the pier, the men would all be walking together. The women would be walking behind them having their own conversations. I think you've been a good influence on these guys."

"I kind of hate to be leaving," Erika said. "This is absolutely the most peaceful and serene place I've ever seen. Guess it's hard for you to leave each time you come here, isn't it?"

Chris looked out over the darkness of the ocean. "You never leave Greece," he said, "and Greece never leaves you. Its impact lasts forever. Times change and the world keeps turning, but these rocks remain constant. You'll really get a feel for the timelessness when we get to Delphi. And the setting up there in the mountains is just magnificent."

"I guess this part of the adventure must end so the next part can begin," Erika sighed.

"And that part must end also so that we can find out what happens after that," Chris added. "Sure hope it involves you."

Erika looked at him and smiled. She squeezed his hand as they turned to head back to the restaurant.

"I'd like that," Erika said. "Like we said before, let's take it easy and see where it goes."

"Patience is my middle name," Chris said.

They strolled back to the parking lot adjacent to Margaret's restaurant. A number of couples, obviously locals, were being seated for their late dinner on the patio. Several couples were walking hand in hand alongside the water, laughing and whispering as Chris and Erika had been doing. A soft breeze kept the fishing boats rocking lightly at the ends of their anchor ropes.

Another magical night, Chris thought.

Uncle Spiro and Aunt Alexandra kissed Ted and Maria and the girls goodnight, and then turned to Chris and Erika. The old lady hugged Chris and kissed him on both cheeks. Her rosy cheeks, beaming smile, and sparkling eyes translated for Erika everything she was saying in Greek to Chris. She did the same with Erika, and offered her the little English she knew.

"*Me to kalo*," she said, offering the traditional Greek farewell. "Is pleasure meeting you."

Erika hugged the old lady tightly.

"And it is a pleasure meeting you," she said. "Thank you so much for everything."

The old lady smiled in agreement in spite of her inability to comprehend everything that was said. Then Uncle Spiro walked up. He held Erika at arm's length and beamed at her.

"*Koukla*," he began, "you brighten up pretty good this old man. We only let you go now if you promise you come back. And soon. I be here long time, but" he added with a wink, "maybe some these people here they don't last so long as old Spiro."

Erika laughed and hugged the old man and kissed him on each cheek.

"Uncle Spiro, I'll bring back lots of memories from this trip, but meeting you will be right at the top of the list. Thank you for everything."

The old man hugged her again and waved goodbye as he and Alexandra walked to their car. They were in their Peugeot tonight instead of the old van in which he normally traveled. An occasion such as this warranted only the best.

Ted, Maria, and Erika re-packed themselves into the tiny confines of the cab of Ted's old truck, while Chris and the girls tumbled into the back. The vehicle had barely left the parking lot before the three in the back were filling the night sky with songs as they lurched their way up the mountain road.

When they finally arrived in Stavroula, Maria sent the girls scampering off to bed. Then she and Ted kissed Erika and Chris goodnight, again thanking Erika for the lovely dinner.

Chris and Erika sat for a while on the porch under another

starlit sky and what was now a waning moon.

"Hate to leave?" Erika asked.

Chris looked at her.

"Normally, I would," he said, "but this time is different. I'm looking forward to getting home and looking behind door number two."

"This has been a magical interlude in a storybook setting," Erika whispered. "Do you think maybe that's what's caused all this?"

"That might be a part of it, but it's just a scenic backdrop. I can imagine getting cross-eyed over you anywhere in the world we might have met. The fact that it was here made it perfect."

"Sounion," Erika corrected. "We met in Sounion, don't forget. And, by the way, you promised to show me what you had written about that place."

"You're right, and I will. Let's plan on it when we get home."

"Do you think you will feel the way you do right now if we were to meet in California or Alabama or somewhere else when we get back? Don't forget, I've had a pretty secure wall around me for a while. You've knocked a lot of that down. But I'm still walking along on eggshells through all this."

"And I'm just the opposite," Chris said, taking hold of her hand. "I lead with my heart. I believe that nothing should be left unsaid. You know that I'm crazy about you. I think out loud, and sometimes it gets me into trouble, but anything I tell you is true and it comes from the heart. The time I spent not knowing whether I'd be around for tomorrow made me aware of how tenuous all this is. I remember reading something once that went, "Of anguish none is greater than the passing of two hearts that never knew each other." Ours have met now, and I want to see what happens next. That's pretty much up to you."

"That puts all the pressure on me then. I'm not sure that's fair."

"It just gives you the keys to the car. You can take it wherever you like and see if it suits you. If it doesn't drive well, we can shake hands as friends."

"Will it be that easy?"

"Who knows. All we can do is go along with what happens

and see if we're both comfortable."

"I guess that's fair enough. You paint a pretty good picture, Greek boy. I think I like being in it."

They rose and Chris pulled her tightly to him. Nuzzling her hair, he became breathless by the overpowering nearness of her. They embraced for a long time before he pulled back and kissed her softly on each cheek. Her eyes remained closed.

"Are you as hypnotized as I am?" she whispered.

"I'm light years ahead of you," he said softly. "But now, I'm off to bed. Tomorrow is a long day. *Kali nihta*, or good night, whichever you prefer."

"I think I like the Greek version better," Erika smiled. "For now anyway."

Chapter Seventeen

Everyone was up early the next morning. Following breakfast, Erika had stripped the sheets from the beds, and had run the last load of their dirty clothes through the washing machine. They had completed most of their packing by nine o'clock. Ted had returned from his early morning visit to the coffee house, and was sitting with Maria and the girls in the kitchen. Chris emerged from his room with his travel bag, placed it in the hallway, and joined them.

"Guess we're just about set," he said, pouring himself a cup of coffee. "Soon as Erika is ready, we're on the road."

"I'll just be a minute," Erika called from her bedroom.

"Well, little brother," Maria began, "has been one good time. The wedding, the visit, and, especially meeting this new person in your life. How you think it goes when you get home?"

Chris smiled and thought a moment.

"Don't really know," he said. "I do know how I hope things turn out, though. I am going to try and take it slowly and just see what happens. And I promise to keep you posted."

Ted picked up enough of the words to know where the conversation was going. He added in Greek his hope that they would be seeing each other.

Erika appeared in the hallway dragging one of her bags. Chris rose to help her.

"Seems like this one grew over the last few days," he joked.

"It has," Erika said. "Bags seem to have a way of doing that while on vacation. I'm not really a power shopper, though. Just a few things I picked up when I visited the Acropolis. I'll shop for a couple of T-shirts and a few other knickknacks when we get ready to leave Athens."

Ted walked down the hallway, picked up the two bags, and carried them to the front porch. Chris went into Erika's room to retrieve her second bag. Maria and the girls joined them on the porch.

"Goodbyes I don't do so well," Maria said, hugging Erika. "Is hard for me every time this brother of mine leaves to go home. This time is more hard because we enjoy so much you being with us. It has been a pleasure having you here. Please know this door always open to you. And please come back to see us. *Na pas me to kalo*," she added, wishing her a safe journey.

Maria then handed Erika a sack with a number of individually wrapped items inside. Erika raised her eyebrows inquisitively.

"Nothing really," Maria assured her. "Just some of the cheese you made and the bread we baked before. Also one box of Greek pastries I made for you."

Erika hugged Maria tightly. "Thank you so much for everything," she said. "I've never been made to feel so welcome, and I've never enjoyed seeing and doing so many wonderful things together. This trip has been absolutely perfect. I hope to get a chance to return some of your hospitality someday."

She turned and hugged Ted in the same manner. "Thank you so much for all you've done and for sharing your home with me," she said. "I will never forget the past few days."

Ted smiled and fumbled through his limited English for enough words to tell Erika how special she was to all of them.

Erika knelt to give the girls a hug, and pulled from her bag a small wrapped gift she had for each of them. Their eyes grew wide in excitement, but instead of opening their presents, they ran to the bottom of the stairs to retrieve two bouquets of flowers they had picked for her. They beamed with pride as they presented their gifts to Erika. She hugged and kissed them both.

"Okay, baby brother, you be careful and take good care of yourself," Maria said, wrapping Chris in her embrace. "And don't stay so long away from your family. *Me to kalo*."

"*Me to kalo*," Chris repeated. He hugged his sister and Ted, and blinked back the tears that were building in his eyes. "Thank you for everything you did. We had a great time. Take good care of my village."

The family walked together with Chris and Erika to their car, and assisted in strategically loading the bags in the trunk and the back seat. When all was in order, Chris and Erika got into the

Toyota and waved a last farewell to them all.

"Don't know how you're going to top that, Greek boy," Erika said as they drove away and began their journey down the mountain. "That was definitely a ten."

"Glad you enjoyed it," Chris said. "Guess the pressure's on to make Delphi shine just as brightly. One thing's for certain, you sure stole a lot of hearts up there."

"You have a wonderful family," Erika said. "I'm jealous."

She was relaxing with one arm propped on her open window and the other stretched across Chris's shoulder, lightly tousling his hair. Gone was her nervous anxiety from their first trip up the mountain. Having made the trip several times over the course of the last few days, she seemed totally at ease now with the drive.

Their return was a backtracking of their journey from Athens. After about an hour of driving through the Argolid plain, they rolled up the windows and switched on the air conditioning, as the sun had begun shining with a ferocity they had not felt in the mountains. Erika smiled as they drove past the road that turned to Uncle Spiro's home and the ruins of Mycenae. Their visit there and the picnic lunch afterwards seemed like a year ago. Much had happened in five days.

The hairpin turns, the drive along the coast, the castle-crowned hilltops, and the endless fields of olive trees were the same as they had been a week before, but they seemed to have a new meaning now. Erika understood the closeness that Chris felt for each of them and for the handful of souls in the tiny village in the mountains that she had come to know. It was clear that all were indelibly etched on his soul, and having seen, felt, smelled, and tasted the true Greece, she was aware that it had woven its magic on her as well. She spoke about it to Chris, and his heart raced at the thought that he had met someone to whom all this was as exciting as it had always been to him. He felt exhilarated.

Erika adjusted her seat to recline slightly.

"Why don't you take a snooze?" Chris asked. "I'll wake you when we get to the Canal so we can grab a bite to eat."

"Not sleepy," she sighed, "just content." She placed her hand again on his shoulder and stroked his hair.

"Tell me about, what was it, Fairhope, Alabama," she said.

"What's it like?"

"It's a place that tugs at the heart," he said. "Small town on the eastern shore of Mobile Bay. Years ago, it was almost unknown except for a few people who moved there to get away from Mobile. It's been almost discovered now, though. It's developed into a mini art colony with some very nice galleries, craft stores, and a few typical tourist stores. Some really nice old homes, Spanish moss draping the live oak trees, quiet lanes to stroll, that kind of thing. It's managed to avoid the tourist crunch so far. Still pretty laid back. After my divorce, I bought one of the old houses, just a small one, at the end of one of those roads where you expect Scarlett O'Hara to come walking around the bend. The live oaks make almost a canopy over the road, and there's only one other house nearby. An old salt lives there who tells some of the best stories you've ever heard. A real renegade. I've got a wraparound porch with a hammock perfect for watching the summer afternoon thunderstorms rumble across the bay. Great views and incredible sunsets. Just me and Baxter, a cat that adopted me about three years ago."

"Sounds heavenly," Erika said reclining in her chair with her eyes closed. "I can almost envision it."

It was almost 1:30 when they crossed the Corinth Canal. Chris pulled into the same roadside *souvlaki* restaurant where they had stopped on their outbound journey. Despite the big breakfast at Maria's, both were hungry and ready for lunch.

Chris selected a table on the patio while Erika went inside to freshen up. When she returned, he was looking over the menu.

"Order one of everything for me," she said. "I'm starving."

"I'm the same," Chris laughed. "And we've been eating continually for five days. Maybe the fact that I'm carrying around all these rocks in my shoes to keep my feet on the ground has something to do with it."

Erika smiled. She reached for his hand and squeezed it.

"I still enjoy hearing that," she said.

"Good," he said. "I want to get a little more mileage out of it before I go to my new material."

Erika laughed again.

The waiter appeared, and they ordered *souvlaki*, the house

specialty shish kabob, and Greek salads. When the waiter's young table assistant appeared with a basket of bread, silverware, and a dish of olive oil, they wasted no time beginning the ritual bread-in-the-oil procedure. They turned their attention to the salads when they arrived, and had finished both plates by the time the *souvlaki* was served. The chunks of pork, green peppers, onions, and tomatoes were still sizzling, and the oregano, lemon juice, and a light dusting of salt and pepper sent their digestive juices into sensory overload. A plate of potatoes, thinly sliced and fried in olive oil, completed the meal. As hungry as they were, they still took their time savoring the experience.

Chris paid the tab when they were finished, and walked to the newsstand to pick up a Greek newspaper and a day-old edition of the *International Herald Tribune*. Erika brought a plastic shopping bag that contained two bottles of water and another roll of the dried figs that she had bought earlier and liked so much.

Chris took another route into town that would lead them to the heart of Athens. They talked about seeing the Acropolis from that same road on the drive back from Sounion less than a week ago. Chris recalled the icy silence that had engulfed them on that ride, and was glad that Erika had explained to him why she had lapsed into her moods. She was as bright and cheery now as she had been morose back then. Arriving at Konstantinou Street, they turned right at the Temple of Olympian Zeus and, in a few minutes, were pulling into the driveway of the Hilton. A polished doorman opened Erika's door, and a parking valet took Chris's keys and handed him a claim check for the car. Bellmen with luggage carts were navigating the loading area, and a tall one with almost no hair on his deeply tanned head loaded their suitcases onto his vehicle. He wheeled his cart onto the elevators, and told Chris he would wait for him there while he registered.

Waiting in line at the reception desk, Chris turned to Erika.

"Well, what's your pleasure, lady?" he asked. "One room or two?"

"Again I'm making the decisions, eh?"

"In this case, absolutely," Chris smiled. "I told you, I'm happy to go slowly with this. Whatever you're comfortable with is fine with me."

The business type ahead of them completed his registration and walked away from the desk speaking into his cell phone.

"Good afternoon," a smiling clerk said.

"Hi," Erika said before Chris could respond. "We'd like a room with a king-size bed for one night," she said to the clerk. "And can we have a bottle of champagne sent up as well?"

Chris stared at her, feeling his heart racing.

"Is that all right with you," Erika asked demurely, looking straight into Chris's eyes. The clerk was consulting her computer for availability.

"I think I can live with it," Chris said.

He handed the clerk his American Express card and waited to sign the registration form.

"Here you are, sir," the clerk said, handing Chris his magnetic door key. "And I will have the restaurant send you up a bottle of champagne. Will you be celebrating an event with us during your stay?"

Chris and Erika remained locked in an eye embrace.

"We've been celebrating one already," Erika said. "This is a continuation."

"Wonderful!" the clerk smiled. "Have a pleasant stay and please let us know if we can be of service."

Chris took Erika's hand as they walked across the glittering lobby.

"The pool looks inviting," Chris said, looking out the floor-to-ceiling windows at the gardens surrounding the Olympic-size pool. "What do you think?"

"I bet I'm in it before you," Erika said.

"You're on," Chris answered.

"Erika!" a voice called. "They told me at the desk that you had checked out a few days ago, but that you would be back here for another stay before leaving Athens. I've been waiting two days for you."

They turned to see who could be there who knew Erika. A man seated in a wheelchair smiled coldly at them.

Chapter Eighteen

The bronze glow that had found a home on Erika's face over the past few days had vanished. In its place was an ashen pallor that had neither color nor emotion. The eyes that minutes earlier had been alive and dancing were now vacant. She stood motionless as a statue, awestruck.

"Paul," she finally said, "what are you doing here?"

"Come now, my dear, that's hardly the way to greet your husband."

Chris was as dumbstruck as Erika. He gazed in silence at the figure in the wheelchair.

Paul was a handsome man, or probably had been at another time in his life. He had a thick head of dark hair that was flecked with gray, giving him the distinguished look of a CEO or doctor. He wore a dark blue sports jacket over a white shirt, open at the collar, and a pair of gray slacks. He had a husky upper body, but his legs were obviously withered from years as a paraplegic. He had a glass that contained several ice cubes and about three fingers of scotch or bourbon or some other dark whiskey. From the look on his face, it was not his first drink of the day.

It was the eyes, however, that gave him a brutally sinister appearance. At some time in his past, they must have been a soft green that shone brightly against his ruddy complexion. But now, especially with their liquor-tinted streaks of red, they glared as coldly as those of a viper. There was much venom behind them.

Chris had seen eyes like that before. They were the eyes of young men he had known, mostly teenagers, who had grown suddenly old fighting a dirty war in a jungle far from home. The vacant, hollow, thousand-yard stares of those who survived and came home, but never really came back. The icy orbs filled with hatred that never mellowed no matter how many years had passed. The eyes that had forgotten how terrible it had been to pull a trigger for the first time, and how easy it had become the last time.

"Erika, you don't seem glad to see me," Paul said, after a long pull at his drink. His speech was on the verge of becoming slurred. "Aren't you going to introduce me to your new friend? He must be a close friend, seeing they way you two were holding hands."

"Paul, I asked you what you were doing here," Erika said, finally regaining her composure.

"Why, I'm here to meet my loving wife, of course," Paul said. "Where is a man's place if not beside his beloved wife. Don't you agree, Mr…?"

"Pappas," Chris said. "Chris Pappas." He stepped forward and offered his hand.

"My," said Paul, ignoring the gesture and downing more of his whiskey, "it appears you've gone the ethnic route this time, my dear. Must be one of the locals. How quaint."

"Paul," Erika began, "this isn't the time and this isn't the place to…"

"Nonsense, my dear," Paul interrupted. "What better time or place for a man and his wife to reconnect. How about a cocktail?" He pushed the lever on the control panel of his wheelchair to turn himself around.

"Andrew," he called, raising his glass, "would you go to the bar and freshen this for me and order a drink for Erika and for her new 'friend'?" The chill with which he emphasized the last word was clearly evident. A tall man in a dark suit approached and took Paul's drink.

"What can I get for you, Madam?" he asked Erika.

"Nothing, Andrew, thank you," Erika said.

"Come now, Erika," Paul said. "What's a reunion without some spirits to toast the occasion? Why don't we get a table in the lobby bar. You can even invite your friend here. What was your name again?"

Chris looked at Paul and said nothing. Then he turned to Erika.

"Chris," she said, "let me have a minute to talk to him. I don't…"

"A minute?" Paul shot back. "Only a minute for a man and his loving wife to re-unite? Surely we have more than a minute's worth of catching up to do?"

"Go ahead, Erika," Chris said. "I'll wait for you on the patio. Are you sure you're okay?"

"Well, it appears that the new friend is a hero as well," Paul said icily. "He's willing to protect you from the man in the wheelchair. How commendable of you, sir."

"I'll be fine," Erika said, taking Chris's hand. "I'll meet you on the patio."

"Ah, again with the holding of hands," Paul added. "This must be more serious than I thought."

Andrew appeared with another drink for Paul. He handed it to him and stepped back out of listening distance from the conversation.

"I'll be on the patio," Chris said. He squeezed her hand and walked across the lobby and onto the patio, where he found a table under the shade of a large poolside umbrella. A waiter appeared and Chris ordered an Amstel.

His brain was reeling from the encounter in the lobby. Her husband? She had said that they were divorced. Was he reappearing to try and persuade her to return, or were they still, in fact, married? The verbal abuse, alcohol-induced or not, that she told Chris she had endured for so long was evident. A hundred other questions and scenarios raced chaotically through his mind.

"Another beer, sir?" Chris looked up from his mental wandering.

"Excuse me?" he asked.

"Would you like another beer?" the waiter repeated.

Chris looked at his empty bottle and glanced at his watch. He had been out there almost a half-hour.

"Yes, please," he said.

He rose from his chair and walked to the glass door opening into the lobby. Erika and Paul were still talking, and Andrew was still standing a respectful distance away. Erika was sitting on the edge of a sofa, and Paul had wheeled his chair next to her. The conversation appeared quiet and low-key. Chris returned to his table and his fresh beer. Could this all be unraveling, he mused? Was this really a fairy-tale encounter destined to end right here?

The door to the lobby opened. Erika came out on the patio and walked over to Chris's table. He rose to meet her.

"Erika, talk to me," he said. "Is everything okay?"

She took his hand, and they sat down. She had a handkerchief in her hand, and Chris could tell she had been crying. The blue eyes still sparkled, but there was much moisture there. The look on her face broke his heart before she uttered the first word.

"Chris," she began, "ever since we met you've been totally honest about everything, but I can't say the same. I need to tell you my whole story." He felt his spirits continue to sink.

"I told you that I was divorced," she continued. "Actually, I filed the papers several months ago and we were scheduled to sign a couple of times, but Paul had each closing postponed. He comes from an old money family of Southern California. His father had inherited quite a fortune, and was connected to enough of the right people to have had Paul exempted from the draft back in the 60s, but Paul was unhappy at home and wanted to get away from the family. He felt that going into the army would be the best way to prove himself. He had always wanted to fly, and fell in love with helicopters. He went through helicopter school and, of course, was sent to Vietnam and assigned to the First Air Cavalry Division. His back was broken and his spinal cord severed in a helicopter accident after only about a month there.

"When he came home, his father was determined that Paul would be successful in his own business. In addition to being an attorney, Paul was a computer whiz, and it was a natural outlet for him. His spinal cord injury would keep him in his wheelchair for life, but it didn't slow him down in his business or in his opposition to the war. That's how he and I met. We ended up starting an information systems management company that became very successful. We also did well in real estate. I worked in the business with him for several years until our relationship began deteriorating.

"I started working for the magazine to be on my own. I was good at what I did, but Paul was relentless in trying to convince me that I couldn't make it without him. I stayed with the magazine despite his pressure, and it infuriated him even more. He even tried to pull strings to get me fired. Like I said, his family is pretty well connected. But, in spite of everything, I'm still working there.

"We had the huge home in one of the canyons above Burbank with a housekeeper, chef, and Andrew to take care of Paul. He didn't want me to attend to him. He came to consider me just a trophy or arm ornament or whatever. Our life was a sham.

"When things at home finally reached an intolerable level, I moved out into a little place in Newport Beach. Living and working on my own has been good for me, but it has made Paul even more furious. His jealousy has become an obsession. When I tried to reason with him and asked him to end our marriage, he laughed and said he'd never agree to it. I've been out for over a year now, and we've been back and forth with the attorneys. Mine says I'm entitled to part of the business since Paul and I started it and ran it together, but I honestly don't want anything except for it to be over. Paul says he'll arrange it so that I won't get a cent, and that's fine with me. He says he'll use everything at his disposal to keep pressuring the magazine to find some reason to let me go. Naturally, I'm worried. I don't know how long they can resist him, and I don't know how far he is willing to go. And now his drinking has become so bad that I'm actually afraid of him.

"Anyway, part of the reason I came to Greece was to sort all this out. I feel confident that I can make it on my own, no matter how difficult he tries to make it for me. He knew I was vacationing in Athens, and told my parents that he was going to try and talk me into coming back to him. I never told my folks all the details about how bad things had become, and they've always held out hope that we'd somehow work things out between us. They told him I was staying at the Hilton and the date I was scheduled to fly back. He was here waiting. You saw the rest.

"Now I've got some very difficult decisions to make. He's going to pull out all the stops in wrecking my life and anyone connected to it. Says that I'll realize that I have to go back to him. The fact that there's no love there doesn't bother him. He feels that he has got to win. Like I said, I'm starting to be afraid of him, especially when he's in the condition he's in now, which, lately, has been most of the time. I know how ruthless he can be.

"What I need to decide is what I can do or where I can go. I don't mind giving up everything that I had with him. I never had that lifestyle before Paul and I were married, and I would be perfectly happy without it now. I thought about moving someplace else, but where would I go? He can pull enough strings to make it very difficult for me to get another magazine job. And he's scared away all but the closest of my female friends and every man who paid me even a little attention. Until now, I thought that I was strong enough to walk away, but he's just now told me what he plans to do if I continue with the divorce proceedings. It scares me, and I don't want to involve you in any of that. I feel like I have to return to the States with him."

Chris stared at her, not believing what he was hearing.

"Erika," he said, "you don't have to do that. And if you do, would things change at home? I'm not a therapist, but I can tell you that he's out to self-destruct. I had a lot of friends who came home from the war in the condition he's in. Some accepted it and worked hard to become the best they could be. Others, like Paul, never did. They needed an outlet for their hatred and self-pity. Over time it consumed them. If he's open to counseling…"

"He's not," Erika said. "He went through several sessions when he came home from Vietnam, but he wouldn't allow the therapist to help him."

"In that case, you've done all you can do. More, even, because you've stayed with him through all this. But you can only do so much. Life's short, and if you ride through it being miserable, you cheat yourself. Especially when you can make a change."

"Chris, you don't fully understand. I'm honestly scared of what he might do. And I couldn't bear the thought of anyone that I was involved with getting caught up in my problems."

Chris took her hands in his.

"Listen to me," he began. "You know you're strong enough and talented enough to make it on your own. If you really feel it's over between you and Paul and the damage is irreparable, tell him so right here. I'll fly back to California with you if you like and be a shoulder to lean on through the signing of the final papers. Then you can decide what you want to do about a change of latitude. If you decide to stay there, I'll go on back home and we'll see what develops between us. If he continues to make your life miserable and you decide that you need to leave, I'll fly you to Fairhope and you can stay with me until you sort things out. That's moving fast, I know, but that's the speed at which things have happened with us anyway. I've got an extra bedroom, so there would be no strings attached. And," he added with a smile, "Baxter wouldn't mind a bit."

Erika looked at him and forced a smile.

"Chris, you're one of the most incredible people I've ever met," she said, "and I love you for extending the offer. But I just can't involve you or anyone else in this."

"But you can't live your life in fear of this man or wondering how he'll get back at you for moving on. If he continues after the divorce, there are courts and restraining orders that deal with those situations."

"Chris, I can't. I just feel like I'd be looking over my shoulder all the time or waiting for the next shoe to drop. He has already gone the private detective route, having someone shadowing me even before I moved out."

"The jealousy and self-pity will consume him even before the alcohol does," Chris said.

"All three are doing a pretty good job already," Erika said, "but I'm scared and I've made up my mind. I'll fly back with him tomorrow. He says if I'll move back home that I'll see him change for the better. I can't see that happening, but he's pretty effective in using the 'invalid war veteran' guilt trip on me. All I can do is thank you for your offer and for the past few days. I will never forget you and your family."

Chris smiled in a vain attempt to mask his feelings.

"Just know that I am in love with you then," he whispered. "I understand that you must do what you feel you must do. Walk in sunshine always."

Erika leaned forward and kissed him lightly on the cheek.

"Goodbye," she said, tears streaming down her face.

She turned and walked back into the hotel lobby to join Paul and Andrew at the bar. Chris walked to the bell stand, where the porters had left Chris's and Erika's luggage. He removed Erika's bags from the cart and walked to where Andrew was standing.

"These are Erika's things," Chris said, handing him the bags, "and here's the valet ticket for her car."

"Thank you, sir," Andrew said.

Chris walked back to the bell stand and, hoisting his own bag over his shoulder, he tipped the bell captain. He walked in a daze across the crowded lobby, and felt his room key in his pocket. Stopping at the reception desk, he dropped the key into the receptacle. He looked one last time at Paul and Erika on their way to the elevators with Andrew walking behind them with Erika's bags. Paul shot a look of smug conquest at Chris. Erika had her eyes fixed on the floor.

The doorman opened the door for Chris as he stepped outside into the city's late afternoon heat.

"Taxi, sir?" the doorman asked.

Chris looked at him as if he didn't understand.

"Uh, no," he said. "No thank you."

He walked away from the hotel, faintly aware that his feet were carrying him towards the Plaka.

Chapter Nineteen

The whump, whump, whump, of the helicopter blades thrashing the air was almost drowned out by the earth-shattering blasts of the mortar and rocket shells as the NVA gun crews in the hills were steadily finding their range. The fiery explosions inched closer and closer as the choppers homed in on the red smoke signaling the platoon's position at the flooded rice paddy nudging against the edge of the triple canopy jungle. Chris and the handful of men who had not been hit began shuttling their wounded buddies to the first chopper that touched down. The dead, wrapped in ponchos, they put on the second and third helicopters, while the platoon sergeant shouted into the radio calling for additional evacuation and air strikes on the ridge line from which the murderous fire was coming. Each explosion was inching closer and closer, until the noise was almost deafening.

Blinking his eyelids into a half open position, Chris realized that the pounding he was dreaming about was actually emanating from his own head. He lay in bed perfectly still, not wishing to move his head even an inch so as not to give the throbbing pain an opportunity to begin anew.

He opened his eyes very slowly and felt the dull thud that spread from temple to temple across his forehead. He was still fully clothed, which told him that he had collapsed into bed immediately upon entering his room. His mouth was as dry as cotton. At least I didn't throw up, he thought. That's one good thing.

Very carefully, in order to not further antagonize the wrecking crew working in his head, he swung both legs out of bed and sat there for a few moments, his head in his hands. Finally, he got up and walked very slowly to the bathroom. If he hadn't thrown up the night before, he felt he could at that moment from looking at the sight in the mirror. He hadn't seen those same swollen, bleary eyes and mattress-destroyed hair in years. He turned on the cold water, and, taking a deep breath, held his head under the faucet as long as he could. The wrecking crew was easing up a bit, but Chris knew that no matter how many cold showers he took, he would have to eat his way out of the hangover. Turning off the water, he leaned both hands against the sink and looked at the dripping head gazing back at him. He towel dried his face and hair, and walked out onto his balcony. The street below was filled with pedestrians and vehicular traffic, and the position of the sun told him it must be late morning. A glance at his watch verified his guess. It was almost 11:00 a.m.

Missed the hotel breakfast, he thought. Have to go out for something on the street.

Walking back into the room, he looked at his duffel bag parked neatly on the luggage stand. The events of the evening then began unfolding for him.

He remembered wandering aimlessly after leaving the Hilton. All he could think about was Erika and her decision to remain with Paul. Their meeting, the trip to the village, the wedding, their time together, the drive back to Athens. They all seemed somehow unreal to him now, as old as the events that led to the dream from which he had just awakened. And they seemed every bit as distant.

Chris remembered snapping back into reality when a taxi driver slammed on his brakes, narrowly missing him as he walked across a busy street near Syntagma Square. He also remembered the cabbie driving away amidst a litany of expletives for which the Greek language has no equal in the world. He directed his steps then back to the familiar scenes on Apollonos Street and the Hermes Hotel.

He registered for a room, but instead of going upstairs he dropped his bag, collapsed into a chair in the lobby, and ordered a beer and a shot of tequila from the bar. After three more rounds, his head felt detached from his body. Chris's friend, the front desk clerk, realized the condition into which Chris was sliding, and asked if he could do anything for him.

Chris had smiled and thanked him. No, he had said, there was nothing that anyone could do.

Chris remembered the stifling feeling that came over him

leading him out into the street away from the smoky confines of the hotel bar. Leaving his travel bag in the lobby, he walked across the street to the coffee house, where he ordered another beer and another tequila. The confused waiter did not understand what tequila was, but told Chris that he could bring him the beer. Chris downed four more during the next hour before stumbling back to the hotel.

The clerk knew immediately that Chris was in the bag. Leaving the front desk unmanned, he walked over to steady him and led him to the elevator. Retrieving Chris's duffel, he accompanied him to the third floor, took his room key, opened the door, and left only after Chris assured him he would be all right. Chris woke up in the exact same position in which he had collapsed into his bed.

After reloading his toothbrush twice in an attempt to brush away the dragon in his mouth, Chris managed to shave without hemorrhaging to death. He crawled into the shower and let the icy water take his breath away. After being revived, he turned the hot handle on to allow himself to soap up and wash thoroughly. He put on a clean pair of jeans and a T-shirt and stuffed his dirty clothes into his duffel bag. His stomach was growling noticeably, reminding him that he had eaten nothing since he and Erika had stopped for lunch the day before at the Corinth Canal. That, too, seemed like light years ago now.

Chris was a little embarrassed when he got off the elevator in the hotel lobby. He was glad the night clerk who had helped him to his room was not on duty.

He walked down the street to a café where he ordered lunch. Afterwards, he stopped at the travel office on the corner, where a young lady confirmed his return flight the next day back to the States.

Returning to his hotel, he sat in the lobby and read another day-old edition of the *International Herald Tribune*. The world had not missed him during the past week. Chris wondered what to do for the rest of the afternoon. He suddenly wanted to be back home. Athens now held many sad memories for him. The city that had been the backdrop for the most intense love affair of his life was now a painful reminder of how that affair had ended. He felt the need to leave.

Chris decided to take the bus to Cape Sounion. The quiet calm and serenity of that place would be a salve for his wounds. Much better, he thought, than the coarse salt that a raucous Athens would rub into them. He went upstairs to his room to put a towel and swimsuit into his backpack in case he might experience an energy rush and decide to take a swim. If not, he would eat an early dinner and take the bus back to town. The thought of a sunset drink made his stomach tighten in protest.

Chapter Twenty

Chris told the desk clerk that he would be going to Sounion, and left instructions for a wakeup call for his room for the next morning. Then he left the hotel and walked through Syntagma Square to the bus stop near the National Gardens. He waited about fifteen minutes before the Varkiza-Vouliagmeni-Sounion bus arrived to load its passengers bound for the resorts along the coast.

He gazed hypnotically out the window as the miles and the sights rolled by, watching but not seeing what was going on. His mind was numbed, anesthetized by the previous night's alcohol with which he had tried to blot out the events of the last week.

After several stops at the beachside communities along the coast road, the bus finally arrived at its turnaround spot at Cape Sounion. In about a half-hour, it would begin its return journey to Athens. Chris would take a later bus.

He shouldered his backpack and stepped off the bus. The sun was still intense despite its late afternoon position in the sky. Chris decided to walk up the hill to the tourist café at the entrance to the ruins of the Temple of Poseidon. He wondered if the memories of his first meeting with Erika would chase him from there, but he was still dehydrated from his binge the night before, and his thirst was winning out over his fear. He trudged up the hill, and sat at a table overlooking the water. The beauty of the setting and the magic he had always felt at that place were wasted on him now. Same ocean, same rocks, same setting, he thought, but an altogether different place. The world was definitely a brighter place when Erika had been a part of his life, even for the few short days he had known her. She's going to take a lot of getting over, he sighed.

He ordered a Coke and a glass of water. When he finished both, he decided to pay the entrance fee and walk into the ruins and onto the point overlooking the ocean. Walking past the temple, he paused to look at Byron's signature. How much had happened since she had walked into his life at that exact same spot a week ago.

Chris eased down on a large boulder and squinted into the sun to view the column where the poet had carved his name over a century and a half ago. I'm sure Byron could have put into words what I feel right now, Chris thought.

A number of tourists were milling about, consulting their guidebooks and lining up their sunset photographs, but Chris was oblivious to everyone and everything around him. His mind was miles away.

The music began as a very low, almost imperceptible glimmer of sound. As it got louder, it suddenly hit Chris like a lightning bolt. He recognized it immediately. It was the melody sung by the gypsy girl in the mountains above his village. The clear tones were somewhat muffled by the wind blowing across the ruins on the cliff where he sat, but the song was unmistakably the one that had mesmerized him and Erika. He jumped up from the rock where he had been sitting and looked behind him. A second lightning bolt struck.

Seated on a boulder about twenty feet away was a woman wearing a blue short-sleeved cotton coverup over a pair of white denim shorts. The breeze was scattering her shoulder length blonde hair across a face with high cheek bones, a slightly turned up nose, and two sparkling blue eyes. Her smile revealed a set of pearly whites that belonged in a toothpaste commercial.

"Hi there," Erika said.

Chris could not speak. He stared at her with his mouth half open and a look of disbelief plastered across his face. Words finally came to him.

"Hi yourself," he smiled. "You come here often?"

"Only when I'm looking for graffiti on Greek temples," she said, "or Greek boys from Alabama." She switched off the tape player.

"Had any luck finding them?"

"Found both, as a matter of fact."

Chris walked over to her. Looking down at her sitting on the boulder, she was again the picture that he had carried with him in his heart and in his mind since the day they met.

"You were wearing the exact same outfit that day," he said.

"I know. It's not by coincidence. Wanted to see if what happened that day might happen again today. I was so scared that I'd missed you and you had already left. I went by your hotel, and they told me that you were spending the afternoon here and flying home tomorrow."

"May I share your rock?" Chris asked.

Erika laughed. "Please do," she said.

Chris drew his knees up to his chest and leaned back against a boulder even larger than the one they sat on. He gazed out at the ocean.

"What happened?" he asked, still looking straight ahead.

"I woke up," Erika said. "We had dinner last night at the hotel. I was in a daze most of the evening. Paul went on and on about the business and what he had planned for me. Told me repeatedly that my future was there rather than working at the magazine, and with him rather than on my own. I didn't sleep at all last night.

"We arrived at the airport around ten this morning for a noon flight to JFK and on to Los Angeles. Standing at the check-in line, it suddenly hit me that I couldn't do it. I couldn't go back to living like that. As scared as I am about the unknown, I'm even more scared of living a lie for the rest of my life. To be honest with you, though, the biggest fear was the thought of not seeing you again. You hit pretty hard, Greek boy."

Chris melted. She was verbalizing things he hadn't even dared dream.

"How did Paul react?" he asked.

"The way I knew he would," she said. "He began with the guilt routine, telling me how I'm walking out on him when he needs me. When I told him that he knew as well as I did that he didn't need me at all, he began the threat approach, ranting and raving about how he would destroy me and my career, and how I'd never work in Los Angeles again. I picked up my camera bag and my overnight case. Everything else I left. I wished him well, shook hands with Andrew, and walked outside and hailed a taxi. He was still yelling and threatening when my cab pulled away. On the ride back into town, I remember feeling freer than I have ever felt in my life. Maybe I'll burn in hell for leaving him, but it's over now and I've made my decision. I had the paper with the name of your hotel still in my purse, and had the taxi take me there. The desk clerk told me where you had gone, and he called a cab for me and negotiated a price with the driver to take me here. So, here I am."

Chris turned to face her. "I'm supposed to be a writer, but I can't find words right now to tell you how I feel," he said. "So where do we go from here?"

"Well, my guide book says that the Taverna Dionysius is the best place around here to escape the heat with a cold soda. Thought I might head over there."

Chris smiled. "Only if you want to be overcharged," he said. "The white awning place at the head of the bay is the neighborhood joint where most of the locals go after their siestas. The old man there does a mean grilled octopus and ouzo. I've got a pocketful of drachmas if you'd like to try it out."

"Sounds wonderful," Erika said, snuggling under his arm.

"How about after that?" he asked.

She was silent for a moment. "After that," she began, "I want to find my way to Fairhope, Alabama. Just for a short while, mind you, until I figure out what direction I'm going in. I'll be traveling light, though. Like I said, I left my bags at the airport except for my cameras and the carry-on. I'll pack a few things when I get back to L.A. Andrew said he'd ship my stuff to me, but who knows. I don't think I snore, and I've been told I am not high maintenance."

"Short time or long time, I don't think Baxter will have a problem with that," Chris said, "and the hammock on the porch is big enough for two. I'll even order a sunset."

They rose and walked hand in hand away from the temple.

"So what did you do last night?" Erika asked as they headed down the hill to the *taverna*. "Did you think about me?"

"To tell you the truth, for the first time in many years, I missed a meal," he said. "I did have a couple of drinks, though."

Printed in the United States
1251200002B/88-1008